CAT
and the
Stinkwater War

Also by Kate Saunders:

The Belfry Witches series

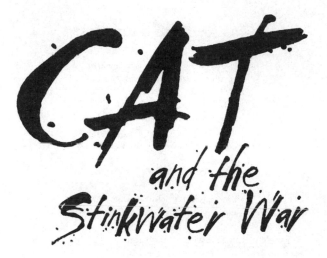

CAT
and the Stinkwater War

KATE SAUNDERS

ILLUSTRATED BY ADAM STOWER

MACMILLAN CHILDREN'S BOOKS

First published 2003 by Macmillan Children's Books
a division of Macmillan Publishers Ltd
20 New Wharf Road, London N1 9RR
Basingstoke and Oxford
www.panmacmillan.com

Associated companies throughout the world

ISBN 0 333 99771 9

Text copyright © Kate Saunders 2003
Illustrations copyright © Adam Stower 2003

Phototypeset by Intype London Ltd
Printed and bound in Great Britain by
Mackays of Chatham plc, Chatham, Kent.

For my son Felix
and our cats,
Trumble, Bing and Boomerang

DRAMATIS FELIDAE
(Cast of Cats)

COCKLEDUSTERS

King Cockleduster the
 Ninth .... Head of the
                                    Cockleduster dynasty

Crown Prince Cockie .... His son and heir

Crown Princess Bing .... The strong-minded wife
                                    of Cockie

Prince Crasho .... The son of Cockie
                                    and Bing

Princess Tarba .... The daughter of Cockie
                                    and Bing

Princess Dollop .... See above

Princess Shallot .... See above

General Nigmo Biffy .... An old soldier and
                                    beloved pet of Cat

Mackerella .... Biffy's daughter

Queenie Eatsmuch .... Biffy's fourth wife – and
                                    pet of Lucy

Everlasting Prendergast ...... A saintly Sardine-
Shouter

Larfing Silex .... Prime Minister

Tuggard Steggings .... A tough fighting tomcat

Elixa Atlas . . . . A tough neutered female

Ploshkina . . . . The fiancée of Crasho

The Donk Brothers . . . . Fighting tomcats

Dr Stoffit . . . . Another Sardine-Shouter

STiNKWATERS

Darson Stinkwater . . . . Head of the Stinkwater clan – and pet of Emily Baines

Sleeza . . . . His chief wife

Vartha. . . . . Their daughter – and heir to the Stinkwater Leadership

Major Mincible . . . . Darson's hench-cat

Pokesley . . . . The turncoat son of Biffy

WiLD ONES

Spikeletta . . . . The queen of the wildcats

Swugg. . . . . One of her eighteen sons

Wizewun . . . . A mystery cat

THE PRINCIPAL CATS

ERIC / GENERAL NIGMO BIFFY

MUFFIN / DARSON STINKWATER

PUSS-PIE / QUEENIE EATSMUCH

TINY / SLEEZA

CAT — THE GIRL CAT

JACKO / MAJOR MINCIBLE

WIDNES / EVERLASTING PRENDERGAST

CROWN PRINCESS BING

TIBS / CROWN PRINCE COCKIE

HAMISH / POKESLEY

SPIKELETTA, QUEEN OF THE WILDCATS

WIZEWUN

1
THE TEMPLE KEY

One Saturday morning, the postman delivered an extremely dirty padded envelope for Cat's father, covered with wrong addresses that had been messily scribbled out. Dad opened it at the breakfast table with his buttery knife. Out fell a small oblong parcel, a grubby sheet of paper and a postcard of a hideous modern hotel somewhere in Egypt.

'Good grief,' Dad said, 'it's from old Katzenberg!'

'But Professor Katzenberg's dead,' Cat said. 'Isn't he?'

'Of course he is,' Dad said. 'I made a speech at his funeral – you don't have funerals for people who aren't dead. He's been dead for nearly two years, so this envelope must have been going round wrong addresses all that time. He must have posted it just before – before—'

'Before the crocodile ate him,' Cat finished for him.

Dad winced. 'We don't know for certain that it was a crocodile,' he said. 'They never found any trace of him except a heap of clothes.' Shaking his head and muttering, 'Poor old thing – he went quite loopy at the end,' he unfolded the sheet of paper.

It was covered with tiny pictures and crazy lines. 'Well, well, well,' Dad said, 'he's sent me his precious map. He swore this map would lead him to the Temple of Pahnkh. And now he's sent it to me!'

Professor Katzenberg had been, like Dad, an archaeologist with a special interest in ancient Egypt. Twice a year (until the tragic incident with the crocodile) Dad and the Professor had gone to Egypt to dig for ancient treasures.

'This map was his life's work,' Dad said sadly. 'Such a waste of a fine brain. He really believed in the legend of Pahnkh.'

'The legend of what?'

Puzzled as he was, Dad smiled. Talking about his special subject always made him smile. 'It's a crazy story from the very dawn of time – long, long before the great pharaohs and the pyramids and the Sphinx. When poor Katzenberg heard it, he couldn't get it out of his mind. Once upon a time (according to this legend), the land we know as Egypt was ruled by a powerful god called Pahnkh. This Pahnkh had a magnificent temple in the suburbs of Ancient Thebes, filled with treasure. He had great powers, but in the end he wasn't powerful enough to keep the stronger gods away from the humans. They forgot Pahnkh, and he was ruined. Or so the story goes.'

'Wasn't Pahnkh human himself?' Cat asked.

'Oh, no. The really remarkable thing about Pahnkh was that he wasn't human at all – he was a cat.'

'A – cat?'

'Yes. In the old story Pahnkh was a black cat, and that's the reason why the Egyptians regarded all cats as sacred. It's a load of codswallop, of course,' Dad said, a little wistfully. 'Heaven knows why old Katzenberg believed it – but he was going very funny at the end, you know. On our last dig he swapped all our tinned food and teabags for a dreadful picture of Pahnkh juggling with the sun and moon. Total rubbish – looked like an ad for Whiskas.'

He picked up the small, hard, oblong parcel and tore off the brown paper. Inside was a white piece of stone, like a miniature brick.

'Very nice,' Dad said, taking a bite of toast, 'but why on earth has he sent it to me?' He picked up the postcard, which was covered with sprawling, untidy writing. 'Dear Julian,' he read, 'my time is running out and I can't wait any longer. Today I will know everything! But in case anything happens to me, I've left instructions to send my map and my piece of alabaster to you. So if you are reading this, I'm afraid

 3

I must be dead. Take very good care of the alabaster – it's one of the Two Keys of the Temple of Pahnkk. Find the other Key and you can enter the hidden Chamber of Gold. Good hunting. Katzenberg.'

Cat was intrigued. 'Did the Professor know he was going to be eaten by a crocodile?'

'Of course not!'

'Then how did he know his time was running out?'

Dad sighed again. 'He probably knew his money was running out. So he decided I had to carry on his mad search for a temple that doesn't even exist.'

'Oh, Dad – why don't you?' Cat thought the legend of the god-cat sounded fascinating.

'I'm not as daft as I look,' Dad said. 'I'd never get funding for an expedition like that – and I'd be laughed out of every respectable archaeological journal in Europe.' He stuffed the map back into the padded envelope. 'Now, what about some more toast?'

'Yes please. And can I give Eric some sausage?'

'Of course.'

Cat cut a piece off her sausage, stripped off the skin and dropped it on the floor beside her chair. Eric, the family cat, came ambling across the room to examine it. He was ten, like Cat (which is old for a cat) and rather stout. His barrel of a stomach was white, and so were his stumpy old legs. His back, the top of his head and his tail were silver tabby. It was hard to connect a comfortable old cat like Eric with a god-cat who juggled with the sun.

Cat helped herself to another chocolate muffin. They were only allowed this sort of delicious, unhealthy breakfast on Saturday mornings while Mum was out jogging. Mum did not approve of unhealthy food. On every other morning, Cat's breakfast was porridge (made with milk so skimmed it was nearly water) and wholemeal toast as rough as a doormat. Mum got annoyed with Dad when he let Cat put golden syrup on her porridge. Luckily, he was the person who did most of the cooking.

It was amazing, Cat often thought, that two parents could be so *different*. Dad was plump and chaotic. Mum was thin and tidy. Her favourite words were 'energized' and 'motivated'. Mum and Dad had told Cat a million times about the day they met (when Dad had accidentally fallen down a manhole in Cambridge and Mum had called the Fire Brigade) but it didn't explain how two such opposites had managed to get married and produce a daughter.

There were a lot of great things about Mum. For instance, she was brilliant at arranging holidays and outings. You could trust her never to miss a plane, a ferry or a motorway exit to Alton Towers. And once you got to a place like Alton Towers, you could also trust Mum to go on all the scary rides – totally unlike

 5

wimpish Dad. But she did sometimes try to run the house like an army boot camp.

The trouble with Mum, Cat decided, was that she was too used to being important. She was Chief Economist at a big city bank called Prewster, Dingle, Huff, where she had three secretaries and gave orders all day long. Possibly, it was sometimes hard for Mum to remember that Cat and Dad were not part of what she called her 'team'. Every morning, before she went to work, she left them both long lists of things to do. Sometimes, Cat suspected, she would have liked to sack the pair of them for being 'unmotivated'.

Dad brought a fresh plate of toast to the table. He picked up the Professor's white brick. 'Poor old Katzenberg,' he sighed. 'Some crook told him this thing was one of the Two Keys to the Temple. He swore it could work magic and grant wishes and I don't know what else.' He leaned across the table and put the 'Key' on Cat's plate. 'Here, you can have this for your museum.'

'Thanks.' Cat liked the look of the stone. When she held it in her hand, it felt hard and cool against her skin.

'Right,' Dad said, putting on his efficient face, 'one more bit of toast – it's nearly time for ballet.'

'Dad—'

'Mum left all your stuff on your bed.'

'Dad, do I have to go to ballet?' Cat hated ballet.

The horrible ballet class had been Mum's idea, to 'energize' Cat's lazy Saturday mornings. 'Couldn't you let me off just this once? Couldn't you pretend we forgot?'

He looked sympathetic, but shook his head. 'Sorry, darling. It's right at the top of my list.' He showed her his list for the day.

It said: 'JULIAN!'

1. Don't let Cat wriggle out of ballet – church hall 11 a.m.
2. Disinfect lavatory brushes.
3. Flea powder for Eric.
4. Pick up dry cleaning.

Cat and Dad both sighed. There it was, in black and white. Even the god-cat Pahnkh, who spun the sun and moon in his paws, would be powerless against the Chief Economist of Prewster, Dingle, Huff.

'OK,' Cat said. She stood up. Her full stomach strained against the waistband of her jeans. 'I'll be upstairs. Thanks for the stone thing.'

Heavy and slow with breakfast, she toiled upstairs to her bedroom. Before she went out jogging, Mum had put Cat's leotard, tights and shoes on top of the duvet. Eric lay in a stout, stripy heap on the leotard. Cat climbed on her bed. She stroked the top of Eric's head in the special, half-scratching way he liked. He stretched luxuriously and jumped to the floor. Cat watched him. For as long as she could remember she had loved watching Eric, trying to guess what went on behind his kind green eyes. When she was very little, she had tried to teach Eric to talk. She was still sure he could understand her.

Eric strolled to the radiator. He warmed his tongue against it, then applied it to his bottom. He raised his head and looked at Cat. His furry cheeks lifted, his eyes narrowed. Yes, he was definitely smiling. Mum did not believe a cat could smile, but Cat and Dad were certain Eric smiled at them. They had made up names for his different sorts of smile – 'Stupid Grin', 'Silly Sweetboy' (Cat's invention) and 'Old Criminal' (Dad's). At the moment, he was Silly Sweetboy, purring loudly. He shifted into what Cat had named his 'chicken-sitting' position, when he sat squat and folded like an oven-ready chicken.

'Silly old Sweetboy,' Cat murmured. 'No wonder you're smiling – you don't have to spend two hours at ballet with nasty Emily Baines.'

Emily Baines was in Cat's class at Bagwell Park Primary, and she lived across the road. Mum thought this ought to make Cat and Emily great friends. Cat could not make her see why this was impossible. Emily was tall and blonde and very pretty, and the most important girl in Mrs Slater's class. She was also (as is often the case with important people) very mean.

Emily had a gang. There were five core members of Emily's gang, who were always Emily's friends. The other girls in the class were sometimes invited into the gang, and sometimes quickly booted out of it. They all longed for Emily's nice moods, and dreaded her sudden fits of nastiness.

There were three girls in Mrs Slater's class who were never, ever invited into Emily's gang. These were Lucy Church, who was very new, Maria Szepinsky, who only spoke Polish, and Cat. Why had Emily decided not to like Cat? Perhaps because she was the most fun to tease. Emily had tried teasing Lucy, but she was too spookily pale and quiet to be rewarding. She had tried teasing Maria, but this was no fun when Maria just grinned and said 'Zenk you'. That left Cat, who blushed plum-purple and was altogether more rewarding.

Dad said, 'Ignore her.' But Cat could not ignore Emily's nasty jokes about her short legs and round bottom. She wanted to disappear when Emily did imitations of her ballet dancing behind the teacher's back. Why did Mum refuse to see that Emily was a total cow? It was hugely unfair that Cat had to spend two hours with this cow every Saturday morning, when she already spent every school day trying to avoid her.

Beside the radiator, Eric stretched and opened his pink mouth in one of his surprisingly enormous yawns. He would spend the rest of his Saturday morning in a variety of cosy places. Just before lunch he would take a stately stroll round the garden to work up an appetite. All his days followed this peaceful pattern.

It would be so nice, Cat thought, to swap places with carefree Eric for one day. With a deep sigh, she tucked the Professor's stone into the pocket of her jeans, and wondered if she had room for one more bagel before ballet.

2

BALLET

Emily Baines was wearing a new pink leotard, white tights and pink ballet shoes. Her mother (who did not go out to work, and apparently existed only to worship Emily) had pinned her hair into a real ballet dancer's *chignon*. She was practising her *pliés*, surrounded by her admiring gang.

Cat huddled into the far corner of the changing room at the church hall. It was vital to be quick. She had to get into her leotard before Emily had a chance to make nasty remarks about her underwear (she had spent a long time that morning choosing her least remarkable knickers). She ripped off her jeans and jersey with trembling hands, and sat down on the bench to heave her white tights over her plump legs.

Beside her, folding her clothes into a neat pile, was

Lucy Church. She gave Cat a quick, uncertain, secret smile and looked away before Cat could return it.

Cat felt her face simmering with the beginnings of a boiling blush. For some reason, the sight of Lucy made her ashamed, as if she had been caught doing something mean. Two months ago, Lucy and her mother had moved into the cramped garden flat next door to Cat's house. They were both small and thin and shy, and always seemed sad. Once they had lived in one of the houses by the Tennis Club, and Lucy had gone to the posh school where the girls wore straw hats. Now her parents were divorced and she was at Bagwell Park Primary.

Lucy and Cat should have been friends, but they had hardly spoken a word to each other. Lucy never made any effort to talk to Cat. She ignored all Cat's attempts to strike up a conversation. In the mornings, when they were both walking to school, Lucy hurried ahead so that she didn't have to walk beside Cat. This was a shame. It would have been so great to have a friend who lived next door. Dad was very good company, but a bald archaeologist was no substitute for another girl.

'Oh, look at Cat!' tittered Emily. 'She's put on her leotard BACK-TO-FRONT!'

Every girl in the changing room looked at Cat. She looked down at herself, and saw that she had indeed put her leotard on the wrong way round – this was what came of hurrying. She stood very still, as if this would make her less visible. If only she could stop herself blushing purple.

'YUK!' Emily said. 'It's gone right up your crack! It'll get lost in all your spare bums — because you do look as if you have about three of them, you know. I shall have to call you MULTI-BUM!'

Everyone except Lucy burst into screams of laughter. They laughed so loudly that Yvonne, the ballet teacher, who was secretly smoking a cigarette outside the fire door, rushed in to see what was the matter. Yvonne was thin and cross, with dyed red hair, and she did not bother to hide the fact that she considered teaching in a church hall beneath her.

'Stop fooling about, Cat,' she snapped. 'And get a move on, you lot — I've got a lunch date at one-fifteen.'

The laughing died away into scattered giggles. There was a general clatter of movement as the girls surged through the swing door into the hall.

Cat stood as still as a statue, biting the insides of her cheeks to stop the tears that were stinging her eyes. She hated Emily. She hated them all. Some of the girls jostled against her on the way out, tittering and hissing, 'Multi-Bum!'

Left alone in the changing room, among the rucksacks and heaps of clothes, Cat sat down on the bench. The Professor's Temple Key was in her hand — she had been about to drop it into her rucksack when

 13

Emily struck. She squeezed it hard, finding something comforting in its cool, crisp angles.

As soon as she joined the class, the laughing would start again. Nobody would laugh out loud, of course, because Yvonne had such a bad temper. But there would be ripples of whispers and little bursts of muffled giggling, while Yvonne shouted, '... and in FIFTH, two-three, DEMI-PLIÉ, two-three – watch those ARMS, two-three—'

A leftover tear escaped and slid down Cat's nose. It fell on the Professor's stone, and lay on it like a pearl. Dad had said this thing was supposed to be magic, and to grant wishes.

I wish Emily would grow a huge, wobbly bum! Cat thought viciously. She imagined Emily screaming as she suddenly grew an enormous bottom. An EVER-LASTING bottom that would grow back if Emily tried to cut it off. This made Cat feel a little better.

For some reason – maybe because she was thinking of the dead Professor's search for the god-cat – a picture of Eric's face came into her head. He was smiling, and his green eyes were full of peace.

In Cat's imagination, she saw Eric's face fading and melting into another furry face – the face of a black cat, with eyes that glowed like yellow searchlights. Who was this? She closed her eyes, and the face of this strange cat filled her head. The glow of his great eyes grew brighter, until they seemed to burn away all Cat's misery and fill her with power.

Her lips moved, and inside her head she heard her voice saying:

'*By the Power of the Temple, I wish I was a votary of Pahnkh!*'

There was a tightness in her chest, like a hand reaching in and squeezing her heart. Cat gasped. Her arms and legs tingled. She felt her back stretching and arching. She was shrinking, shrinking, shrinking, until her tights and leotard lay around her in a floppy heap. The Professor's stone became warm, then hot, then burning. She dropped it with a cry that came out in a long, ragged mew.

This could not be happening. Cat collapsed in the empty folds of her leotard. She felt as if she had been carried miles and miles in the bosom of a great wind. She knew that she was very small. The changing room had become a huge cavern filled with enormous jumbled shapes. Everything had a blue tinge, like a faulty video.

But not being able to see as well as usual did not matter. Cat's ears were suddenly so sensitive that she could hear a whole world of new noises – deep rustlings under the floor, whispers she could half-understand, murmurs and cries and chirps and squawks. A carnival of sound. Normally, all you could hear during the ballet class was the clunking piano music on Yvonne's tape player, and Yvonne's loud voice. Cat could still hear all this, but it was distant and unimportant. A bird chirped outside the window. The sound made Cat hungry, and also angry — *stupid, irritating, delicious bird!*

And the SMELLS! Cat turned her head, and the smells surged around her, so vivid that she could almost hear them. She caught the smell of Emily Baines on Emily's pink trainers, and was amazed to feel hairs standing on end all over her body. Her back arched. Her mouth gaped open and let out a furious yowl.

There was a cat in the room.

It was her — she was a cat.

She held out her hand — and saw a dainty orange paw. Inside her head she could still think human thoughts — but her human thoughts seemed to be roped off in a corner, and they kept getting mixed up with the thoughts of a cat. It was incredible. What did she look like? The only mirror in the room was far away above the sink. Her legs were gloriously strong and springy. With one graceful leap, Cat was on the edge of the sink, balancing as easily as a tightrope walker in a circus.

In the mirror, she saw a small cat of brilliant marmalade, with big eyes as pure green as two emeralds. Her striped orange neck still had the velvet fatness of kittenhood, but her limbs and tail were long and slender. She had often wondered how it felt to have a tail.

Now she knew it was like having an extra limb to hold out for perfect balance.

And she was adorable. The human Cat had wavy brown hair and round brown eyes, and was perfectly nice-looking, in an ordinary sort of way. But there was nothing ordinary about the flame-coloured creature she saw in the mirror. Cat had heard that female gingers were extremely rare, and was proud of being so special. For the first time in her life, she knew how it felt to be beautiful. She whooped with delight (it came out as a deep 'miaow') and jumped off the sink, landing neatly on Lucy's rucksack.

This felt FANTASTIC – how many people got a chance to take a holiday from their own bodies, and do things their dull old arms and legs had never dreamt of? Cat leaped and twirled and sprang, revelling in her lightness and freedom. She dashed madly round the changing room, running along the tops of the pegs and making daring dives on to the heaps of folded clothes. She found that she could stretch and squeeze her ginger body like a concertina. Being a real cat was every bit as wonderful as she had imagined. She jumped and frisked until she was breathless.

Then she sat down to think. Before she knew what she was doing, she was licking between her sharp little claws, with a tongue as rough as sandpaper. As the astonishment wore off, she began to worry. Even if she had known how to wish on the Professor's stone in reverse, it had fallen right to the bottom of her rucksack, among all the crisp packets and sweet papers. She stuck her whiskery little head into the opening – wrinkling her nose at the huge smell of the old banana-skin she had forgotten to take out yesterday.

Out in the church hall the piano music stopped.

Yvonne's voice said: 'What on earth is keeping Cat Williams? Cat!'

Cat heard the door of the changing room creaking open. She tried to hide herself by scrambling into the rucksack – but even as a cat, she was betrayed by her sticking-out bottom. She squeaked as she felt Yvonne's fingers closing over her back.

Yvonne muttered, 'How did *you* get in?'

Cat squirmed through Yvonne's fingers and dropped down on the stone floor. The darned toes of Yvonne's shabby pink ballet shoes towered above Cat like a pair of tugboats. The mountain that was Yvonne loomed forward. Cat had the very odd experience of being picked up. Now she realized how light she was – how small and helpless. Humans were dangerous. Yvonne was being perfectly gentle, but she smelt all wrong. Cat wriggled in alarm. Yvonne's grip tightened. She laughed, and whisked back into the hall.

'Look what I found! Does this young lady belong to any of you?'

Instantly, a crowd of twenty-five girls, all loudly cooing, surrounded her.

'Aaah! Isn't she SWEET?'

'Oh, the little DARLING!'

'Can I hold her?'

'Me first! Me first!'

Cat-the-cat trembled. There were too many of them. They were too big. Their smells were too confusing. Their big, busy hands flapped at her. She cowered against Yvonne's bony chest.

'Stand back,' Yvonne said. 'I think she's frightened.'

In the wilderness of strange smells, Cat smelt something safe. She jumped blindly towards it – and the human part of her saw that she was jumping into the arms of Lucy Church. Lucy had a lovely safe smell. The touch of her hands was confident and gentle. Cat's small body juddered with a purr of relief.

'She certainly likes you,' said Yvonne – who was smiling for once, and who had apparently forgotten all about her missing pupil.

Lucy's voice was quiet and uncertain. 'I have a cat. Perhaps she smelt her on me, and decided I was friendly.'

'Yes, that must be it,' said the horrible, show-offy voice of Emily Baines. 'Give her to me – I'm sure I smell of my darling little Muffin.'

Lucy did not want to give up the cat, but Emily expected to be obeyed. Cat saw a giant pair of hands

 19

reaching down to her, with fingers like the bars of a cage. The smell they carried was spiked with terror. She let out a scream, and her claws dug into Emily's skin.

'OW!' shrieked Emily. 'The little – OW! – get her off me!'

Yvonne firmly scooped Cat off Emily. 'Okay, that's enough. I'll put her outside.'

Lucy asked, 'Shouldn't we call the RSPCA?'

'She'll find her way home,' Yvonne said breezily. 'They always do.'

Emily scowled, rubbing the red scratches on her hands. 'She's got a nasty character. Muffin would never attack anyone.'

'Come on girls, back to the class!' called Yvonne.

Tucking Cat firmly under one arm, she strode through the porch of the church hall towards the street. She jerked open the door and dropped Cat on the pavement. The door slammed shut, and Cat found herself alone in a vast, bewildering outside world.

3
SMELLS HAVE FACES

Trying hard to be brave, Cat sat down on the cold pavement and wondered what to do next. The mysterious stone sent by Professor Katzenberg was inside the church hall. If she couldn't get her hands — paws — on it, she might never be human again. Even if she went home, her parents wouldn't know her. They would think their daughter had been kidnapped. And when they were searching for their kidnapped daughter, they wouldn't have time to notice a strange marmalade cat. A terrible picture came into Cat's mind of her poor, grieving parents giving her to the Blue Cross. She would be adopted by strangers, and spend the rest of her life mewing for food and being turfed out of armchairs.

She held out her front paws. Maybe she could still

hold a pencil. Then she could write a note to Mum and Dad – something like, 'Help! I am your daughter!' But even if they believed her, what could they do for her, beyond buying her a collar and a basket?

Cat was on the point of howling with despair when she remembered Eric. Of course – Eric was a cat. He would understand her, and she had always thought he looked wise. She must go home at once to consult him. Luckily, her home was only round the corner. On all four shaking legs, Cat began to trot along the pavement.

It was the sort of journey that cats – real cats – did all the time, without turning a whisker. For this amateur cat, however, it was a terrifying obstacle course. The smells were a terrible distraction. They were as distinct as faces – each smell had its own personality. She smelt several other cats, and knew just from their smells that two of them were clever, but one was rather daft. She smelt the hurry and greed of the rats down in the sewers. She flitted past dustbins and smelt rotting food.

The house where the Great Dane lived absolutely reeked of him. Cat's heart thumped uncomfortably. The dog himself was watching her through the downstairs window. The human part of her heard two deep barks. The cattish part heard a shout that she could almost understand – like a voice calling something in a foreign language. She scurried past him as fast as she could, very glad that the humans never allowed this gigantic beast out on his own.

A fly buzzed past Cat's nose. It had a tempting, meaty whiff. Before she knew what she was doing, she found herself smacking the fly between her two front paws and throwing it into her mouth. The human part of her was disgusted. Yeuch – she was actually *eating a fly!* It struggled against her tongue, buzzing loudly. She knew she should spit it out, but she couldn't. It was too delicious. And anyway, who cared about flies? They were crafty customers who deserved everything they got.

Cat stopped. She shook her small orange head several times, to clear it. Since when had she thought flies were 'crafty'? She crunched the delicious, disgusting treat in her pointed teeth, and worried that the cat part of her was starting to take over. If she stayed like this for too long, would she turn back into a girl who behaved like a cat? Would she find herself curling up on the radiator during classes, or trying to rub herself against Mrs Slater's legs?

She was outside the pub – the Admiral Tunnock. It was owned by the parents of Marcus Snow, who was in her class at school. Children were welcomed at the Admiral Tunnock, and Cat had often eaten here with Mum and Dad. She crept to the door, hopefully sniffing a richly cattish smell. This must be Widnes, the famous pub cat. Everyone loved Widnes. He was a very fat, very friendly black-and-white with a luxurious purr like the engine of a Rolls. Cat would have loved to talk to this kindly old soul, but there was no sign of him.

A butterfly fluttered clumsily past Cat's nose like a drunken autumn leaf, and she forgot all about Widnes. Cat-the-cat mewed with delight. The snack of her dreams had fallen out of the sky – the cat version of a bag of crisps or a slab of chocolate. It was brilliant being in a world where the air was full of free snacks. She leapt up and wrestled the butterfly to the ground. She stuffed it into her mouth without bothering to kill it, and the wings went on fluttering for ages.

The human part of Cat was horrified.

The cattish part thought of the dead butterflies in a glass case at home, and wondered if they would still be nice to eat – could a butterfly go stale?

Suddenly, in the middle of crunching the last piece of wing, she felt the air around her turn freezing cold with danger. There was a terrible smell behind her, of darkness and wickedness. This smell had a wild, cruel face. Cat turned round fearfully and found herself looking into the evil, acid-green eyes of Emily's black cat, Muffin.

Muffin was a skinny, long-legged animal. He had rusty splodges of brown along his back, and a mean, narrow face.

'Young female – you are POACHING!'

Cat nearly choked. He had spoken to her! A cat had spoken to her, and she understood what it was saying! His voice was nothing like a human voice. You could hardly say it was a voice at all – it was a series of huffs and yowls and silent thought-waves.

'That wingthing is MINE,' hissed Muffin.

'Wingthing?' stammered Cat. 'Oh, you mean the – oh, I'm sorry – I'm afraid I've swallowed it now.'

'Your smell is strange to me,' Muffin said. 'I can't put my claw on it, but I don't like it. Where do you come from?'

'Number 18.'

'LIAR!' snarled Muffin. 'I know of no such land!'

'But it's not a land, it's just down the street,' Cat said. All her new cat-senses (and some of her old human senses) told her that Muffin was dangerous. She tried not to look scared, but every hair on her body was standing on end. 'Eric lives there,' she said desperately. 'Do you know Eric?'

'Be silent,' Muffin said, with a feline grin that bared his fangs and chilled Cat's blood. 'I know who sent you. Well, well. News travels fast.'

'But nobody sent me!'

Muffin flicked his tail like a whip. 'Tell that fat, useless, so-called King not to bother looking for what he'll never find. And if ever I catch you stealing on my land again . . .' He paused, and his claws shot out of his black paws, 'I will KILL you.'

 25

Cat turned and ran along Tunnock Avenue like a bolt of lightning. She did not stop until she had hurled herself through Eric's cat flap in her own back door. Gasping for breath, she collapsed on the kitchen floor. The house was empty. The terror began to fade. Muffin had not chased her. Neither had his horrible smell. The only cat-smell around here belonged to Eric. Feeling stronger, Cat sat up. She knew Eric would protect her.

Mum's briefcase was under the table, wafting out her lovely smell of soap and safety. The human part of Cat wanted to cry.

The cat part of her suddenly picked up an even more gorgeous smell – liverish, sour, rotting.

She followed it. It was coming from Eric's bowl, on the floor beside the washing machine. Cat's stomach rumbled. She had eaten a big breakfast, but that had been when she was human. As a cat she'd had nothing but a bluebottle and a butterfly. She stuck her face into Eric's food and began to eat greedily.

The cat flap thumped behind her. A furious cat voice shouted: 'I say! This is a bit much! Who are you? And what are you doing in MY land?'

It was Eric, and he didn't know her. Cat tried not to be hurt, but it was painful to see the beloved stripy face glaring at her so angrily. She ran across the floor to hug him, remembered she was a cat and licked his paw instead.

'You've been at my grub too!' Eric gasped, in a voice of outrage. 'Of all the cheek!'

'Eric, it's me – Cat – your human owner,' Cat blurted out. 'You have to help me – I've been turned into a cat and the wishing thing is still in the church hall, and—'

'What?' shouted Eric. 'What in the Sardine's name are you talking about? Get out of this kitchen immediately!'

Once again, the girl part of Cat wanted to cry. 'Eric, it's ME! Why don't you recognize me? I know it's sounds crazy – but you're my only hope.'

'I warn you, young female,' Eric said hotly, 'you might think I'm old and doddering, but I still have a trick or two under my collar.'

'I'm Cat! Please believe me!'

'How did you get in, anyway?' demanded Eric. 'My smell must be wearing off.'

'Look, I'll prove I'm your human girl,' Cat said. 'I gave you a bit of sausage this morning.'

Eric was startled, but still very suspicious. 'So? Anyone could have guessed that.'

'Yes, but I also know what you did with it,' Cat said. 'I saw you hiding it in the airing cupboard.'

The old tabby-and-white cat twitched in amazement. 'You've been spying on me!'

Cat couldn't think who on earth would bother to

 27

'spy' on her cat, but there was no time to go into it. 'Look, Eric, ask me anything. Test me.'

'Test you?' Eric frowned. He began to pace up and down on the kitchen floor, sometimes bending his head to sniff at a crumb.

'All right,' he said. 'Name my greatest treasure.'

She had not expected this. Did cats have treasure? Then, in a flash of inspiration, she thought of Eric's favourite toy. 'Your ringing ball.'

'Correct!' cried Eric. 'This is ASTONISHING! What does it look like?'

'Yellow plastic, very scratched,' Cat said promptly.

'And when did I get it?'

'My fourth birthday,' Cat said. 'I gave it to you to cheer you up, because you were in disgrace.'

'Correct!' shouted Eric. 'But before I make up my mind about you, here's a question no one but my humans could answer. Are you ready?'

'Ready,' said Cat.

'WHY was I in disgrace?'

'Mum caught you on my party table, licking the butter.'

'By the Great Fish, she's right!' Eric sat down suddenly, in a furry heap of amazement. 'Well I never! Can you really be my smallest human tin-opener?' He sniffed. 'There's certainly something odd about your smell.'

'Yes,' said Cat, 'that's what Muffin said.'

'Eh?' Eric was alarmed.

'You know — the cat from number 33. Thin and black, with brown—'

'Oh, my dear little opener!' gasped Eric. 'That was DARSON STINKWATER himself!'

'Who?'

The old cat opened his mouth to explain, then changed his mind. 'You don't need to know, since you're really a human. But while you're a cat, keep away from him.' He was stern. 'Do you understand?'

'OK.'

Eric sighed, and shook his head. 'Well, this is a nice tin of fish, I must say. You'd better tell me how it all happened.'

Cat told him the whole story, ending with her terrified dash through his cat flap. Eric listened with deep interest.

'The huge dog didn't mean any harm,' he said, when she had finished. 'He was probably only trying to warn you about Darson Stinkwater. He's quite a good sort.'

'Oh. Aren't cats and dogs enemies?' Cat asked.

'We used to be,' Eric said, 'but the dogs have been on our side since the War with the Birds.'

'What's the War with the Birds?'

Eric was shocked. 'Didn't they tell you at your human school? Well, we haven't time for a history lesson now.' He squared his furry shoulders in a businesslike way. 'We need to change you back into a girl.'

'I don't think it's possible,' Cat said forlornly, 'unless I can find a way to break into the church hall and get my rucksack. And I don't see how, while I'm stuck as a cat. Oh, Eric, what shall I do?'

Eric kindly patted her tiny paw with his big one. 'Now, now. Brace up. We'll think of something.' He smiled. 'By the way, I don't know why you keep calling me "Eric".'

'Isn't that your name?'

'Oh, no. That's just the noise the humans make when my food is ready.' He stood up very straight. 'Allow me to introduce myself properly. General Nigmo Biffy, at your service.'

'General?'

'Retired now, of course,' the 'General' said wistfully. 'But in my day, I was known as the "Hero of Sprew".'

'Sorry?'

'The Battle of Sprew,' the old cat said proudly. 'We went to war with Frelish of Stinkwater (great-grandfather of Darson) over drain-sniffing rights. And I personally dealt with Red Podge of Kleenit Meadow.'

Cat noticed that he was looking modest, and said, 'Well done.'

Just as she had known that 'wingthing' was cattish for butterfly, she somehow understood that 'Sprew' meant Pole Crescent, 'Kleenit Meadow' meant the launderette on the corner, and 'Red Podge' was the ginger tom who lived there. If she had not been so worried about being stuck as a cat, she would have been fascinated.

She asked, 'What should I call you?'

'Just "Biffy" is fine,' said Eric/Biffy.

His pointed ears suddenly swivelled round to the sound of Mum jogging in at the front door. Before either cat could decide what to do, Mum was in the kitchen. She saw Cat. She crouched down and gathered the small marmalade cat in her arms. Cat purred, rubbing her furry cheek against Mum's tracksuit.

Unfortunately, Mum had not picked her up to stroke her. 'Good grief, what's this cat doing here?' she muttered to herself. 'I told him that flap would attract every stray in the neighbourhood. Don't worry, Eric – I'll get rid of it.'

She jerked open the back door and dropped her disguised daughter on the garden path outside. This was too much to bear. Cat burst into the cat version of tears – a series of pitiful mews. Biffy's portly body squidged through the flap to join her.

'Poor kitten,' he purred kindly. 'Tail up.'

'Oh, Eri – I mean Biffy. What am I going to do? How can I get that stone thing back when I'm a cat? Oh, I wish the professor had never sent it.'

'Shhh!' Biffy hissed sharply. 'Human approaching – you'd better keep out of sight.'

Still mewing, Cat scuttled under the big laurel bush at the edge of the lawn. Peeping out from under the

 31

leaves, she saw that the approaching human was Lucy Church. Cat's heart gave a leap of hope. Lucy was carrying Cat's rucksack, which was stuffed with all her belongings – her trainers were sticking out at the top.

'That's my bag!' she whispered to Biffy, forgetting that Lucy couldn't possibly hear her. 'The professor's stone is in there – right at the bottom!'

She watched as Lucy knocked on the back door. Oh no – now Mum would know she had missed ballet. Once she had solved the problem of turning back into a girl, she would have some major explaining to do.

Mum opened the back door. 'Hi, Lucy!' She liked Lucy, and wanted a best friend for Cat almost as much as Cat did herself. 'I'm afraid Catherine's out at the moment.' (Nobody but Mum ever called her Catherine.) Her sharp eyes took in Cat's rucksack. 'Hang on – wasn't she with you at ballet?'

Even with her powerful cat's ears, Cat had to strain to hear Lucy's soft voice. She was saying something about the extraordinary way Cat had suddenly vanished, leaving behind every stitch of clothing.

Mum was worried, and also annoyed. 'Well, thanks very much for bringing all this back,' she said. 'I can't think what that naughty girl is playing at – good grief, even her underwear's in here!' There was enough of the human left in Cat to be deeply embarrassed when Mum held up her discarded knickers.

Goodbyes were said. The back door closed. Lucy glanced around to make sure nobody was looking, then she climbed nimbly up the trellis and jumped into her own garden next door. The girl part of Cat was impressed. Lucy, who seemed so delicate and weedy, climbed almost as well as a cat.

Biffy had noticed this too. 'Nice legwork for a human,' he said approvingly. 'Now, let's see if we can grab back that magic thing.'

The two cats crept across the garden path to spy through the cat flap. Cat saw Mum in the kitchen, looking very thoughtful. One by one, she took every single thing out of Cat's rucksack, muttering and shaking her head. Out came the ballet clothes and street clothes. Out came the old crisp packets and apple cores, and the forgotten notes from the headmistress about parents' parking. Last of all, out came Professor Katzenberg's piece of alabaster. Cat held her breath as Mum examined this curiously, and seemed to wonder what to do with it. Finally, she put the stone on the kitchen table. She stuffed Cat's clothes into the washing machine.

The doorbell rang. Mum – still unusually thoughtful – picked up her handbag and left the room.

'It's the organic vegetable man,' Cat told Biffy. 'She always talks to him for ages.'

'Perfect,' Biffy said. 'I'll pop in and fetch your stone.'

Cat wanted to warn him about breaking the

precious, troublesome stone. She need not have worried. Biffy went to the cooker and pulled down a tea towel that was hanging on the door. He dragged this across the floor. With surprising grace for one so stout, he leapt on to the kitchen table. With his nose and his paws, he pushed the Professor's stone across the table. Cat gasped when he nudged it over the edge, but it fell neatly on to the tea towel.

Biffy gave her a smile of triumph and began to push the stone across the floor to the flap. Very neatly, he flipped it through the cat flap, and Cat had to dodge to avoid it hitting her on the nose. Her heart sang with relief – she could be a girl again.

'That was brilliant!' she cried, as Biffy's striped head appeared at the flap. 'I've never seen anything so neat!'

'Nonsense – nothing to it – used to do stuff like that all the time when I was a fighting tom.' Biffy could not help looking pleased. 'By the Great Fish, it's a pity you've got to turn back into a human. You haven't heard any of my anecdotes. Ah, well – time and toads wait for no cat.' He scrambled out into the garden.

Cat rested one orange paw on the stone. She stared into Biffy's wise, grape-coloured eyes. 'Thanks for helping me,' she said. 'I'd never have done it without you. And – and it's been lovely to meet you.'

She felt a little silly saying this, when she had lived

with Eric/Biffy all her life, but the kind old cat seemed to know what she meant.

'Likewise,' he said. 'And it would be nice if you could ask the other humans not to put down any more of that awful dried food with green bits.'

'I'll do my best,' promised Cat. 'And I'll get you some Meaty Sticks as a thank-you present. A whole packet.'

'Now you're talking!' said Biffy, who loved a Meaty Stick.

She licked his paw. 'I'm going to miss being a cat.'

Now it was time to work the magic. Strangely, Cat seemed to know what to do. She lay her whole body on top of the alabaster brick. It grew warm underneath her furry stomach. She felt her mind emptying, until there was nothing in it except the strange, solemn face of the black cat with yellow eyes. And she found herself saying:

I seek permission to leave the Temple, oh great one!

The magic crashed over her like a great wave.

Her arms and legs swelled and grew, tingling as if an electric current were rushing through them. She felt her skin grow chilly as her fur melted away. She found herself lying, in a big, fleshy human sprawl, on the concrete path.

Biffy was staring at her, with his white-and-tabby fur standing on end and his tail puffed out like a

 35

feather duster. Now she knew what a cat looked like when it was astonished.

She knelt to hug him. 'Thank you! And please don't be scared – I'm still the same!' Her human voice was loud and booming in her strangely dull ears. Suddenly, there were almost no smells.

And suddenly, Cat realized she was stark naked.

Mrs Pecking, the old lady who lived above Lucy, was staring from behind her net curtains.

'Oh, no!' groaned Cat. Trying to cover as much of herself as possible with her two hands, she pulled open the back door and belted into the kitchen – clumsily, because she was not used to having hands or feet again. She was going to be in big trouble with Mum for missing ballet. She decided she had better dash straight upstairs for some clothes, before she made the trouble any worse.

Unfortunately, she had forgotten about the organic vegetable man. When Cat crept out of the kitchen, she found the front door wide open and Mum talking to the vegetable man about GM crops. The man looked past her at Cat's nude body. Seeing his startled face, Mum turned round.

'*Catherine!*' she gasped.

4
A DEATH-BASKET

Cat couldn't think of an explanation – and Mum wouldn't have listened to her anyway. She thought her daughter had gone crazy.

'Look, I'm not mad,' Cat protested, for the hundredth time.

Mum said, 'I don't know how else to describe a child who strips naked and runs through the streets.'

'But nobody SAW me. Honestly!'

'Nonsense. Of course they saw you. I'll never be able to look the neighbours in the eye ever again. What on earth made you do it? I suppose I ought to send you to a psychiatrist.'

'Come off it, Harriet,' Dad said. 'We don't need some bearded German to tell us the kid hates ballet. She was only playing you up.'

Mum was relieved to think that Cat had stripped naked because she was 'playing up', and not because she was a lunatic. But playing up was serious enough. The punishment was no crisps, chocolate or videos for a month. The only bright spot that day was a phone call from Yvonne, hinting that there was a long waiting list for her ballet class. Very crossly, Mum told her that Cat would not be returning.

'Ghastly woman,' she said afterwards. 'I'd better find you another Saturday activity – perhaps French, or chess . . .'

Even French couldn't possibly be as bad as ballet. Cat went to bed cheerfully, not minding that Mum had sent her upstairs far earlier than usual. The whole experience of being a cat had been very tiring. Cat yawned loudly. She put the Professor's stone in her jewellery box and fell into her soft, human's bed.

This had been an incredible day. Though she didn't fancy being a cat again, she wouldn't have missed the experience for the world. Some of it had been very frightening – for instance, her meeting with Muffin, whose real name had struck terror into her brave old cat. But some of it had been lovely. She had danced and played in a cat's body, and glimpsed a secret world no other human knew about. It made her see the family pet in a startling new light. For the rest of that weekend, Cat made a special fuss of Biffy. She kissed and stroked him. She let him watch television on her knee (she didn't always allow this because his head got in the way), and she spent a good bit of her pocket money on the packet of Meaty Sticks she had promised him.

'Don't let that smelly old moggy shed hairs all over you,' Mum said.

Cat was glad Biffy could not understand these insults – she knew now that cats understood very little human speech. She wished she remembered the cat language. She longed to talk to Biffy again. There were so many things to ask him. Who was Darson Stinkwater? Why was everyone so scared of him? She had forgotten, while she was a cat, to tell Biffy about Darson's mysterious message – something about a king who was fat and useless. What could it have meant?

Cat had enough sense not to use Professor Katzenberg's stone again – she now knew that the cat-world was full of danger. But she wished she could talk to someone. A best friend who was a cat would be better than no friend at all.

By the time Cat arrived at school on Monday morning, the whole of Mrs Slater's class knew that she had dashed through the streets in the nude.

'Nothing but a little heap of clothes,' Emily told her audience of girls in the playground. 'Yvonne said she couldn't *imagine* what she was wearing. She'd even left her *knickers.*' She saw that Cat was listening, and added, 'She must have looked like a wobbly pink balloon!'

Everyone laughed, of course. Even the boys. Cat ate her lunch in a remote corner of the table, trying to ignore the titters and the loud remarks about nudity and knickers. She couldn't explain what had really happened, because she had no one to talk to in the whole world. Lucy looked a bit sorry for her, but she did not try to stand up for her.

After this long, lonely day at school, it was good to get home and hug Biffy (Cat could no longer think of him as Eric), who was waiting for her on the doormat. He followed her into the kitchen, where Dad was cooking pasta.

'Hi, Dad,' said Cat.

'Hi, darling,' said Dad. 'Good day?'

'Fine, thanks.' It had not been 'fine', but Cat never liked worrying him.

'Any homework?'

'Just reading. I did it at lunch.'

The rest of the afternoon and evening followed the usual routine. Cat ate supper. She talked to Dad about the terrible email argument he was having with another archaeologist. She watched the television. Mum came home (in a fairly good mood, though she couldn't resist asking Cat if she had managed to keep all her clothes on). At half past eight, Cat went to bed.

She dreamt that she was on a beach, building a giant sandcastle. It was so big that Cat could walk through the giant gates into a sandy tunnel. The tunnel suddenly collapsed, crushing all the breath from her body, and she woke to find Biffy sitting on her chest. His nose was pressed against hers, so that all she could see was a pair of green eyes staring in a striped face.

She gently shoved the heavy cat aside and switched on her bedside lamp. It was one o'clock in the morning. Cat sat up, blinking to clear her eyes. Biffy patted her leg with one paw, still staring.

'All right,' Cat whispered. 'I get the message. You want to talk to me.'

There was no point in saying anything else to him until she was a cat again. Cat climbed out of bed and fumbled in her jewellery box for the alabaster stone. She knew that the matter must be important — Biffy would not expect her to take such a risk for nothing. She told herself she was only doing her duty because she owed Biffy a favour. But when her fingers closed around the cool white marble, her veins were tingling with excitement. Now that she had an excuse, she couldn't wait to be a cat again.

The stone grew warm in her palm. Once again — never really doubting that it would work — Cat allowed the strange face of the black cat to take over her mind, and asked permission to enter the Temple.

Professor Katzenberg's stone dropped to the floor, with her empty pyjamas. This time the process of turning into a cat was quicker, as if her body had learned what to do. Cat lay panting on the carpet for several minutes, separating the new sounds and unplaiting the tangle of smells. Gradually, her cattish eyes made out the jumbled shapes of her bedroom furniture.

'Sorry about this,' Biffy said, 'but it's an emergency.'

'What's happened?' asked Cat — trying to imagine what a cat's emergency could possibly be.

'It's GONE!' Biffy groaned. He scratched his ear fiercely with his back leg. 'Someone has betrayed the hiding place, and the Tabernacle is empty! The House of Cockleduster lies in RUINS!'

'Sorry, Biffy — but I've no idea what you're talking about.'

The old cat sighed. 'In real terms, it means we may never hunt again by the Drains of Fatoom.' He shook his head sadly. 'The Stinkwaters are denying everything, of course. But we know they stole it. Our spies say they were singing victory songs all last night.'

'Look, I don't understand a word — WHO stole WHAT?' Cat was so impatient that she mewed out loud. The sound shocked both cats back into their senses.

Biffy sat up very straight, like a china ornament. In a deep, slow, serious voice he said:

'*The Blessed Sardine.*'

This meant nothing to the human part of Cat, but the cattish part felt a solemn thrill. She almost bowed her head, without knowing why. 'The – what?'

'IT,' said Biffy. 'The Great Thing. The Good Blessing and Giver. I realize that you are only a human, but you must try to understand how important it is to us. I knew those Stinkwaters were plotting something – I know they're planning to invade us! This is border-country, and we've had skirmishes almost every night. They'd never have DARED before they had the Sardine. It's gone, and we need your help!'

Cat jumped across the carpet to lick his furry cheek. 'Of course I'll help you – I'll never forget the way you helped me.'

'I was hoping you'd say that,' Biffy said. 'But I must warn you that it could be dangerous. We may have to drop you behind enemy lines.'

'Why? Who's the enemy? Is there a war?'

'You'll know everything when we get to Parliament,' Biffy said briskly. 'Follow me – quiet as a fish!'

'We humans say "quiet as a mouse",' Cat said.

'Do you? Can't think why. A mouse makes a hell of a racket. Come along.'

The two cats stole through the sleeping house and out of the cat flap. At night, the garden was a mysterious new world, full of fleeting shadows and

 43

dangerous smells. Cat stuck close to Biffy's tail. Her cat's body was tingling with energy. This was all a little scary. But it was also adventurous and exciting. Did the local cats really have a Parliament – or was this all part of some mad dream?

The Parliament was in the Jessops' garage, behind the back gardens. Biffy led Cat round the great bulk of the Jessops' car, and she could not help letting out a mew of surprise. The floor, the shelves, the bonnet of the car and the top of the chest freezer were covered with cats of every colour. Dozens of pairs of green eyes stared at Cat through the unlit gloom.

'Here she is!' cried Biffy, 'and she says she'll help us!'

There were cattish murmurs of approval, and encouraging smiles from the nearest cats. When her cat vision had got used to the darkness, Cat found that she recognized several of the furry shapes around her.

She knew 'Tibs', the rather clumsy tortoiseshell from the house on the corner. He was small and skinny, with paws that looked too big for the rest of him. Cat smiled at him kindly.

'Bow!' Biffy hissed in her ear.

'What?'

'Bow to the Prince! My dear, that is Crown Prince Cockie, Heir to the Sardine Throne!'

'Oh, sorry.' Cat bowed to Tibs-the-Prince.

He gave a mew that was the cat version of a giggle.

'Are you really a human? What's it like to have those big silly legs?'

The cat beside him (a pretty black female with a white triangle over her face) slapped his nose with her paw. 'If you can't talk sense, shut up!' she spat.

'That's his wife,' Biffy whispered to Cat. 'The Crown Princess Bing. You'd better bow again – she's the one who hunts the mice in THAT family!'

Cat bowed to the Crown Princess, whom she had often seen sitting on the dustbin outside Number 12. It was amazing to discover the hidden lives of all these familiar cats.

Princess Bing stared at Cat. 'So this is the girlcat. She looks rather small. But she could be very useful. Thank you, girlcat. You are welcome.'

Her husband, Prince Cockie, was lying half asleep with his chin resting on his paws. Princess Bing gave him a hard nudge with her bony elbow.

'What? Oh yes. Welcome,' said the Prince.

'It's very good of you to help us, dear,' said a kind voice in Cat's ear. She turned to see the elderly tabby cat from next door – 'Puss-Pie', who belonged to Lucy. 'I have a human female about your size.'

Of course, 'Puss-Pie' was not her real name. 'This is Mrs Queenie Eatsmuch,' said Biffy. 'My third wife, as a matter of fact.'

'WHAT!' choked Cat. She had no idea her old pet had one wife – let alone three.

Mrs Eatsmuch laughed. 'Your FOURTH, Biffy. Do keep up.'

There was tittering among the lady cats nearby.

'Sorry, Queenie.' Biffy moved on to a tubby ginger, also well known to Cat. His human name was 'Trousers', and he was often to be found purring on a gatepost in Pole Crescent.

'Our Prime Minister,' Biffy said, 'Larfing Silex.'

Cat decided to bow again. It was strange bowing to someone whose chin she had tickled.

'Hello,' chuckled Larfing Silex, jolly as ever.

'Girlcat,' said Princess Bing, 'my husband's father, the King, is too ill to leave his basket. We will hold the meeting without him. First, you must meet my children.'

'Oooh, that's a compliment.' whispered Mrs Eatsmuch, very impressed. 'She doesn't let them meet just anyone!'

'My son, Prince Crasho,' announced Princess Bing. She smacked the head of a large, sulky young tortoiseshell beside her. 'Don't SLOUCH, Crasho. And these are my daughters—' She stopped suddenly, glancing around crossly. 'Where are they? Come out, girls, for goodness sake. The human won't bite you!'

Out of the shadows crept three very pretty and very shy black-and-white cats, smiling timidly at Cat.

'My daughters,' said Princess Bing, 'the Princesses Tarba, Dollop and Shallot.'

The three shy princesses made little delicate movements with their heads and front paws. Cat somehow understood that this was how lady cats curtseyed.

'They're so refined!' whispered Mrs Eatsmuch.

Another lady cat hissed, 'Unlike their mother!'

'Well, Bing's not royal,' whispered Mrs Eatsmuch. 'She's a STRAY! The Prince broke his mother's heart when he married her.'

'The Cockledusters always marry beneath them,' sniffed the other lady cat. 'If you ask me—'

'Stop that gossiping!' snapped Princess Bing. She jumped on to an old paint tin, knocking off the Prime Minister. 'Cockledusters, you know why you're here. We can no longer avoid a WAR with the Stinkwaters. They have STOLEN the Blessed Sardine!'

A great mew of fury made the concrete walls echo.

'We'll start with a prayer,' Princess Bing went on. 'Shouter Prendergast – if you please.'

Cat was surprised. Did cats have vicars? And who – or what – did they pray to? A deep, solemn hush fell over the garage. Out of the crowd of cats stepped an extremely fat black cat with a thick band of white round his throat.

'Widnes!' Cat cried joyfully. It was the dear, cuddly old fellow from the pub.

Biffy was full of respect. 'No, my dear. This is the Reverend Everlasting Prendergast – our Sardine-Shouter.'

 47

The Sardine-Shouter gave Cat a friendly grin. Then he started the shouting. 'BLESSED SARDINE! Where are you? Show your smell, so that we can steal you back and exterminate the Stinkwaters! Bless this strange human girlcat who has promised to help us. And bless our King, Cockleduster the Ninth – who keeps SAYING he's going to the country. Thank you for leaving him with us in our hour of need, and for putting off gathering him into your bosom for such a LONG TIME. It's really very generous. Goodbye.'

'Goodbye,' muttered all the cats – this was obviously what they said instead of 'Amen'.

Cat was fascinated to hear about the King. Was this the same one Darson had mentioned in his message? She somehow knew that 'going to the country' was cattish for dying.

Shouter Prendergast bowed to the Prince. 'And how is your royal father tonight?'

'Same as ever,' the Prince said, in a bored voice. 'He keeps making noble death-basket speeches, but then he ruins it by asking for a bit of cheese.'

'Hmm,' said Larfing Silex, 'going to the country doesn't seem to have spoiled his appetite.'

Cat noticed that Biffy was worried, and that some of the younger cats were impatient when the King was mentioned.

'Tell him to make up his mind!' shouted a voice from the back of the crowd. 'A king in a basket's no use to us! If we're going to rescue the Sardine, we need LEADERSHIP!'

There were snarls of agreement.

'I'll give you all the leadership you need!' shouted Princess Bing.

'She certainly will,' said her husband. 'Take my advice and let her get on with it.'

Ignoring him, the Crown Princess turned back to Cat with a gracious smile. 'Human thing, sit down,' she said. 'Let me explain why we need your help.'

Cat sat down. She was a little scared of the bossy Princess, but the solid, furry forms of Biffy and Mrs Eatsmuch, on either side of her, were very comforting.

'First, you must know about the Blessed Sardine,' said Princess Bing. 'It was given to my husband's family during the War With the Birds – but it's much older than that. The Sardine gives our family of Cockleduster the power to rule in peace and goodness.'

'Excuse me,' Cat began.

There was a universal gasp of shock. Biffy hissed in her ear, 'Don't interrupt her – but if you do, say "Your Highness".'

'Your Highness,' Cat said, 'what exactly do you rule? I mean, where is your nation?'

Princess Bing's triangular face looked surprised. 'Where? Why, right here! All the land between

 49

the Green Mountain in the north, the southernmost tip of the Windy Terribles and the Wastes of Tidebolt.'

'Oh,' Cat said. 'Thank you.'

The human part of her understood that this meant the roads between the reservoir, the flats in Hopton Street and the other side of Tunnock Avenue. This did not seem a very large or beautiful country to go to war over, and Cat had always thought the human local council 'ruled' it, if anyone did. But she didn't want to offend the Crown Princess.

'If the Stinkwaters have got their filthy paws on our Sardine,' Princess Bing said, 'we're all lost. They will use the POWER of the Sardine without the GOODNESS. This must not happen!'

'It must be difficult for a human to take in,' Everlasting Prendergast said, in his fat, kindly voice. 'Some day, little girlcat, you and I will share a delicious bowl of dirty rainwater and I'll give you the whole history. For now, all you need to know is that the Stinkwaters are EVIL. If they have the Sardine — oh, PRAISE to its SCALES—'

('Goodbye,' all the cats muttered reverently.)

'—just a few Stinkwaters will hog all the hunting and sniffing rights, and make the rest of us into their SLAVES!'

'They're already occupying part of Woshnab,' Biffy said hotly. 'We should have driven them out right away, instead of letting them hang about terrifying decent kittens!'

'Well, it's no use looking at me,' Crown Prince Cockie said crossly. 'My paws are tied until Father goes to the country.'

'This is a National Emergency,' declared the Prime Minister, Larfing Silex. 'We'll get the King's permission to send out extra patrols. He'll have to say yes – this is WAR!'

The air around Cat hummed and vibrated. All the cats were purring deeply, which was their version of cheering.

'Human thing!' cried Princess Bing. 'Can you stand by while the Stinkwaters make us their slaves? Will you help us?'

'Of course I'll help,' Cat said. 'But what on earth can I do?'

'General Biffy says you attend a human school with the Keeper of Darson,' said the Princess.

'Keeper?' Cat realized she meant Emily Baines. 'Oh yes, she's in my class.'

'Darson would never be silly enough to hide the stolen Sardine in his garden,' said Larfing Silex. 'But he might hide it in his human's house. And you're a human. So you could just pop in, without making any cats suspicious.'

Cat's heart sank. Larfing Silex and Biffy looked so pleased with themselves, she hadn't the heart to tell them that Emily was her worst enemy. She would never get herself invited into Emily's house in a million years – but how could she disappoint those furry faces? 'It'll be her birthday soon,' she said slowly. 'Maybe I can go to her party.'

'Splendid!' cried Biffy. 'I knew you'd help us. Nine cheers for – for – we'd better give you a proper name. I shall call you Girlcat Verripritty, with the rank of Acting Captain. Only "acting", because you're not exactly a real cat.'

'Nine cheers for Acting Captain Verripritty!' ordered Princess Bing.

Once again, the Jessops' garage vibrated with feline cheers. Cat felt very proud, and determined to find a way into Emily's house. How wonderful, she thought, if I managed to save the Blessed Sardine!

'It's a good name for you,' said Biffy. 'You're such a pretty little thing – if I were a few years younger, I'd marry you.'

A cattish giggle ran through the older lady cats.

'Get along with you!' chuckled Mrs Eatsmuch. 'You haven't been married in years.'

Biffy gallantly bowed his head. 'Ah, Queenie, I could soon show you there's life in the old cat yet!'

Cat was very curious. 'Biffy, how many times have you been married?'

'Seventeen,' Biffy said, with a nostalgic smile.

'SEVENTEEN!' Cat was staggered. 'You mean you've had SEVENTEEN wives?'

'That's right, Captain Verripritty. I have twenty-eight sons and fifteen daughters living locally – and that's jolly useful in the present emergency.'

'Biffy's children make up a whole regiment of the Cockleduster army,' Mrs Eatsmuch said proudly. 'My sons are all officers.'

Cat now saw why her parents felt guilty about not having Biffy neutered. He was a one-cat population explosion.

'Permission to speak!' shouted a loud, rude voice at the back of the crowd.

'Granted,' said Princess Bing. 'Step forward, Tuggard Steggings!'

A handsome black tom with white paws pushed to the front. 'How do we know that the human thing isn't one of THEM? How do we know she's not a Stinkwater SPY?'

'Damn your impudence!' Biffy shouted furiously. 'She's MY human. That should be enough!'

'She might be your human,' said Tuggard, 'but that's no guarantee. Look at Pokesley – your SON!'

The name caused a flurry of cattish gasps and mews.

Biffy's green eyes had darkened dangerously. 'That cat is no longer any son of mine. How dare you mention his name?'

'Sit down, Tuggard,' said Princess Bing. 'Pokesley is

 53

a traitor – but I would trust my royal life to General Biffy.'

'Thank you, Your Highness,' Biffy said. His voice shook a little.

Mrs Eatsmuch was whispering in Cat's ear. It was very muffled and ticklish, but Cat caught the main point – that Biffy's son Pokesley had joined the Stinkwater side. To her surprise, she knew the traitor – his human name was 'Hamish' and he lived in Sedley Terrace with Mr MacWheesh, the dentist. Cat had often stroked him in the waiting room.

Tuggard Steggings had not finished. 'For all we know, Pokesley could be hiding the Sardine – I vote we INVADE his garden!'

Some of the young male cats cheered.

'Rubbish,' growled Biffy. 'Darson will be guarding the place, and we won't stand a chance. I vote we send in a special undercover agent!'

Cat knew what she had to do. It was easier than making friends with Emily Baines, but just as unpleasant. 'I could get into the house as a human, then change into a cat,' she offered miserably. 'All I have to do is make a dental appointment.' She hated going to the dentist – Mr MacWheesh had such a hairy nose.

'But that's too risky!' cried Everlasting Prendergast. 'Can we allow this little girlcat to walk right into the jaws of the enemy?'

'I'm not scared,' Cat told him firmly.

'By the Fish, you're a brave little creature,' Biffy said, leaning forward to give Cat's whiskers a lick. After that, she felt she could face anything.

Princess Bing was smiling. 'The Stinkwaters haven't got a trained human,' she said. 'We'll keep the girlcat a SECRET – they must never find out.'

'The Stinkwaters always find out!' shouted Tuggard. 'How did they know where to look for the Sardine? If you ask me, it was an INSIDE JOB!'

This was a shocking idea. The cats began to shout and squabble and panic, until Princess Bing's sharp voice cut through the racket.

'Tuggard, for the last time – SHUT UP!' she hissed. 'We know who told them about the hiding place – POKESLEY, who is no longer one of us. Nobody else will tell the Stinkwaters about the human girl.' She smacked the head of her husband. 'Wake up, Cockie. It's time to present her to the King.'

'Ah, yes, the Sardine's Anointed!' sighed Everlasting Prendergast.

Cat forgot her worries about Emily and Mr MacWheesh. She was longing to see the dying King.

A silent, soft-footed crowd of cats led her out of the Jessops' garage and through the back gardens of Tunnock Avenue. In the dark, Cat couldn't tell exactly where she was. She thought she recognized the patio at Number 26. An old couple called Mr and Mrs Watson lived here, and they owned an ancient tortoiseshell cat who had not been seen out for months. Was this Cockleduster the Ninth? Cat's heart thudded with excitement. She joined the long, silent line of cats diving through the Watsons' cat flap one by one. Biffy held the flap open with his mouth, so they wouldn't make a noise. It was extraordinary, Cat thought, that so many creatures could be so quiet.

It was still more extraordinary to be creeping through the Watsons' house. What on earth would Mum and Dad have said, if they had seen her? They thought their daughter was completely human, and fast asleep at Number 18.

The cats crowded into the dark kitchen. There – in a huge basket, lying on a knitted blanket – lay King Cockleduster the Ninth. He was very fat, and lay very still. Prince Cockie reached out a paw and prodded his father's bottom. The King let out a loud snort and slowly opened his eyes.

'Still alive, then,' the Prince muttered. 'Just checking.'

Cat could not stop gazing at the toys scattered around the royal basket. He had balls, mice, bells, cushions and a cloth carrot stuffed with catnip. Suddenly, Cat saw these cat-toys as dazzling, priceless treasure. The human part of her remembered when her class had been to see the Crown Jewels at the Tower of London. The squeaky mice and ringing balls now looked as beautiful and as precious as the Queen's rare diamonds.

'Come here, girlcat,' croaked the old King, when Biffy had told him about Cat. 'Come close, so that my tired eyes can see you.'

Cat trotted up to the death-basket, feeling very shy and solemn.

'The time draws near,' whispered the King. 'The fight will be hard, but the Sardine has sent this human thing to help us. I can go to the country in peace.'

The human part of Cat suddenly wanted to cry. It was heartrending to think of the death of this fine old cat. She noticed, however, that the other cats looked rather bored. The Prime Minister began licking his marmalade stomach.

'BLESS you all!' rasped the King. 'My son!' He held his shaking paw out to Prince Cockie. 'Rule them kindly and wisely, as I have tried to do.' He fell back on his blanket with a feeble, expiring gasp. There was a long silence. Was he dead?

The royal whiskers moved. All the cats turned their ears towards him, to hear his parting words.

He whispered, 'Do I smell Cheesy Snacks? I could just fancy one.'

'They're bad for you,' said Princess Bing.

'Oh, give him a Cheesy Snack,' sighed Prince Cockie. 'It obviously won't kill him.' The King's humans had thoughtfully left out a little bowl of snacks. The Princess picked one up between her teeth and carried it to her royal father-in-law.

Outside the flap, there was a sudden, sharp mew. Every cat (except the King, loudly crunching his Snack) became very still.

'Don't worry,' said Biffy, 'it's only Mackerella. I put her on lookout duty. She's one of my daughters,' he added, to Cat. 'And she's a good girl — just had another very bonny litter.'

Mackerella put her tabby-and-white head through the cat flap. 'The Stinkwaters have finished their evening song, Father, and I've got to get home to feed the children.'

'All right, my dear,' Biffy said. 'Run along.'

'She's a treasure, that Mackerella,' Mrs Eatsmuch whispered to Cat. 'Her mother was one of the Pish sisters, you know.'

Cat felt her mouth stretching into a tremendous yawn. Her brain was too scrambled with new impressions to take in any more cat family trees. She followed Biffy out of the Watsons' kitchen, her tail drooping with exhaustion. She was so sleepy that she hardly knew how she got home.

On the landing outside her bedroom, Biffy gave Cat's face an affectionate lick.

'Thanks for helping us,' he said. 'Now, pay attention Captain Girlcat — when I need to contact you, I shall place my ringing ball on your pillow. I'll tell the other cats that will be our sign. Got that?'

'OK, Biffy. Goodnight.'

Somehow, Cat managed to change herself back into a human, pull on her discarded pyjamas and fling herself into bed. Her final thoughts, before sleep washed over her, were full of worry. Talk about Mission Impossible – she had promised to go to the dentist *and* make friends with the meanest girl in her class.

5

NUDE AT THE DENTIST

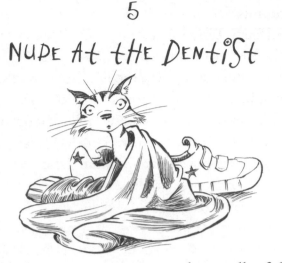

Cat woke up next morning to the smell of burnt toast. Bright sunlight hammered at her red-and-blue striped blinds. After her strange, dark adventure among the cats, everything looked incredibly normal. By the time she had hurried into her clothes and pelted downstairs, Cat had almost decided the whole thing had been a crazy dream.

But Biffy was waiting for her, and he seemed to guess what she was thinking. As soon as Cat sat down, he jumped up on the table. His ringing ball was in his mouth.

'Good grief,' said Dad, 'what on earth is that cat up to?'

Biffy dropped his ringing ball into Cat's plate. He gave her a long, searching look. Cat stared back, trying to send thought-waves that she remembered her promises.

Dad gave Biffy's bottom a smack with the oven glove. 'Off!'

The stately old cat dropped back to the floor, nearly knocking over the milk.

Cat cleared her throat. She would start at once, before she had time to get nervous. 'Dad, could you make me an appointment with Mr MacWheesh?'

'Mmm?' Dad was reading a letter, frowning with deep concentration.

'I need to go to the dentist,' Cat said miserably.

This was surprising enough to take Dad's attention away from the letter. Cat had never asked to go to the dentist. She usually had to be dragged there. 'Why? What's the matter?' he asked.

'Um – I think – er – one of my fillings might be – sort of – cracked.' Cat knew she was useless at lying. She stared down at her organic wholemeal toast, ordering herself not to blush magenta.

Luckily, Dad had gone back to the letter he was reading. 'Poor you,' he said. 'I'll see if Mr MacWheesh has a slot after school.'

Cat's heart sank. 'Thanks.'

'This is ridiculous!' Dad shouted suddenly. He waved his letter. 'I'm not paying. It's as simple as that.'

'Not paying what?' Cat asked.

'It's old Katzenberg again. He's an even bigger

nuisance when he's dead, apparently. This letter is from the manager of that hideous hotel in Egypt. It's taken him nearly two years to find me, but he expects me to pay the Professor's bill! The old nutcase named me as his next of kin!' Dad was cross because he was sad. Cat had only met the Professor when she was a baby, but she knew Dad had been very fond of his old teacher. Katzenberg had borrowed money shamelessly, he had eaten Dad out of house and home, he had even set fire to his curtains once – and Dad had always forgiven him.

'That's just his way,' he would say, when Mum complained. 'It goes with the genius.'

Since Katzenberg's death, Dad had not been able to hear the word 'crocodile' without his eyes misting over. He missed the Professor keenly.

In morning school, Cat thought about the eccentric old scholar, and wished she could talk to him – what a shame he had not lived to see what his stone could do. She wanted to ask Professor Katzenberg about the black cat's face she saw in her mind when she transformed. Could this be the mighty Pahnkh? Was she receiving messages from the ancient god-cat? And if so, what could he possibly want from her?

'Cat! Wake up! Earth to Cat Williams!'

Cat blinked. The whole class was looking at her and giggling. Mrs Slater stood in front of her with her hands on her hips. Cat's class teacher had a youngish face, very short grey hair and loads of earrings, and she was normally kind and easy-going — but she couldn't stand people not concentrating.

'Cat, what have I just been saying?'

'Er . . .' Cat tried to clear her head of cats, professors and sardines. 'You said the dinner money's going up.'

'That was half an hour ago. Next time you bring your body to school, try to remember your brain!'

Mrs Slater had a nice turn of phrase, and the class laughed appreciatively.

Cat felt the heat pumping into her face. This blush was a tremendous one. It blazed all through maths, and was still simmering at morning break. In the playground, Emily and her gang had bagged the good bench beside the drinking fountain.

'Here comes No-brain,' Emily said.

'No-brain!' sniggered the gang. 'Earth to No-brain!'

Normally Cat would have put her head down and run away as fast as possible. Now, however, she couldn't help remembering her promise to the cats. She had to be NICE to Emily Baines, which was like being nice to a rattlesnake. How was she supposed to do it? *Hi, Emily — would you like to insult me until I start crying?* In desperation Cat began the Niceness by giving Emily a friendly smile.

Emily saw, and gasped with outrage. 'Don't you pull disgusting faces at me, Cat Williams!'

 63

'But I wasn't – I didn't mean—' Cat didn't know how to explain. Obviously, her idea of a friendly smile looked like everyone else's idea of a fiendish leer. Emily herself was too dignified to pull faces, but her gang did it for her, crossing their eyes and sticking out their tongues until Cat hurried away, mortified. Being nice to Emily was a waste of time. It would have to be Plan B – getting the truth out of the traitor Pokesley.

When she got home, Cat found that Dad had made her a dental appointment for four-thirty that afternoon. Mr MacWheesh's surgery was just around the corner in Sedley Terrace. At a quarter to four, Cat marched grimly up to her bedroom to prepare for her first mission.

She needed clothes that could be put on in a hurry. This was very important – she might need to change back into a dressed human very quickly. After rejecting two sweatshirts with tight necks and one pair of jeans with fiddly buttons, Cat chose her blue tracksuit and her trainers that fastened with Velcro. She wore nothing under the tracksuit (which felt rather strange, like wearing pyjamas in public) and no socks inside the trainers (which would make her feet smell cheesy, but never mind). She placed the Professor's alabaster brick in her pocket, and she was ready.

Dad looked at her oddly when she came downstairs.

'Are you sure you don't want me to come with you?'

'No thanks,' Cat said firmly – that would ruin everything.

'But you've never gone to the dentist by yourself.'

'Dad, I'm not a baby. And it's only round the corner.'

'Don't forget your coat.'

'I don't need a coat.'

He glanced at the clock on the wall. 'You'll be far too early.'

'I like reading the comics in the waiting room,' Cat said. 'Bye.'

She was nervous as she hurried towards Sedley Terrace. Pokesley might be dangerous. She might be ambushed by evil Stinkwaters who knew no pity. If she didn't keep her head, she might be seriously hurt, or even killed. And if the Stinkwaters killed her, what would happen to her dead body? Would she be a dead kitten, or a dead human? Would she be buried in a flowerbed, or would poor Mr MacWheesh be arrested for murdering her?

Get a grip, Cat told herself crossly. She'd never find the Blessed Sardine if she gave in to panic.

Mr MacWheesh lived in a square white house with a green door. There were two doorbells, one marked 'Surgery', the other marked 'Private'. The MacWheesh family, and the cat they knew as

 65

'Hamish', lived in a flat above the surgery. Cat pressed the 'Surgery' bell. Just as she had hoped, Mr MacWheesh was busy with someone else — she could hear the dismal whine of his drill behind a closed door. She told the receptionist she had got the time wrong, and she didn't mind waiting. She went into the waiting room.

Mr MacWheesh's waiting room was a depressing place, furnished with a few hard armchairs, a fishtank and a pile of shabby magazines. Cat looked at the clock. She had twenty-five minutes before her appointment. Just as she was deciding to sneak past the receptionist and search for Pokesley, in strolled the cat himself.

Like his father, Pokesley was mostly white, with blobs of silver tabby. He was smaller and thinner than the portly old general. Cat watched him wandering round the room, sniffing at the skirting boards. When he turned and trotted out into the hall, Cat was ready.

She crouched down so that the receptionist would not see her over the desk (and how silly this would look, if anyone did happen to see her). Holding the alabaster stone in her pocket, Cat followed Pokesley up the stairs. She needed to change into a cat as soon as possible, in case she ran into Mrs MacWheesh, or the two big MacWheesh sons. Luckily, the family part of the house was quiet. Besides the drill downstairs, Cat could hear a Hoover on the floor above. If she did this properly, nobody would ever know.

Pokesley whisked through a door on the landing. Cat followed him. She was in a spare bedroom, very quiet and bare. The window was open. Cat didn't think the opening was large enough for a cat, but Pokesley poured himself through it and hopped briskly off the sill. Cat saw him jump from the sill to a drainpipe, from the drainpipe to the roof of the extension, and from the roof to the lawn. There was not a second to lose.

Cat carefully put her stone in the middle of the flat, hard spare bed – she wanted to be able to find it in a hurry when her mission was completed. Would it work again? She took a couple of deep breaths. Into her mind came the glowing yellow eyes and black face of the mysterious cat. Once again, she asked to be admitted to the Temple. Magic surged through her veins.

She was a cat. Her little red-and-orange paws scrambled over the empty tracksuit and trainers. The human part of Cat was nervous, but the cattish part knew exactly what to do. Her body stretched like a piece of melted wax until it was thin enough to slide through the open window. Breathlessly, she took Pokesley's route down into the back garden. Where had he gone? Cat sniffed the air for the traitor's furtive, guilty smell, and caught it streaming out of the place behind the tool shed.

Pokesley, his tail twitching, was busy burying something in the loose earth.

'Stop right there!' Cat hissed at him bravely.

The treacherous cat jumped nervously and began to tremble like a jelly.

'Show me what you're burying!' ordered Cat. 'And turn round slowly with your paws up!' This was how the police spoke on television. Now that they were face to face, she was not afraid of Pokesley – she could tell that he was a coward and a fool, but not at all dangerous.

'Yes, yes!' squeaked Pokesley. 'Don't scratch me! Don't bite me!' He dug up the object he had been burying and turned round with it in his mouth.

It was not, as Cat had hoped, the Blessed Sardine. Pokesley was holding a yellow ringing ball, identical to Biffy's favourite toy.

'Just my savings,' he whimpered. 'You wouldn't steal a poor little cat's bank account!'

'I'm not interested in your savings,' Cat said. 'You know what I want. Tell me where it is, and we can end this stupid war.'

'I don't know what you're talking about.'

Cat sighed. 'Don't play games with me, Pokesley. The Blessed Sardine has been stolen – and you know where it is!'

Pokesley was getting braver, and this made him cocky. He let out a snigger. 'I might, and I might not. Tell my father to come himself next time.'

Cat noticed that though his voice was angry, Pokesley's eyes looked sad. She tried to make her cat's voice friendlier. 'You could tell me, and come home to the Cockledusters — I'm sure they'd forgive you.'

Pokesley shook his head miserably. 'I can't. I'm a Stinkwater cat now.'

'Why?' Cat demanded. 'Don't pretend you like them! You're terrified of them, just like everycat else. Oh, Pokesley! Why did you fall out with Biffy?'

'He wouldn't promote me,' Pokesley said sulkily. 'My OWN FATHER wouldn't let me be an officer, because he said I was a complete PLAPP.' (Cat understood that 'plapp' was rather coarse cat slang for 'idiot'.) 'Darson Stinkwater says he'll make me a captain when he becomes King. So there!'

'I'm sure Biffy's sorry he called you a plapp,' Cat coaxed. 'Come home!'

'Who are you, anyway?' Pokesley sniffed at Cat suspiciously. 'There's something dead funny about your smell.'

'PLEASE save the Sardine and come home.'

'I don't know where it is,' Pokesley said, with a silly titter. He began to lick crumbs of soil from his paw. 'Only Darson and Major Mincible know — and if they didn't tell ME, they certainly won't tell YOU!'

Suddenly, quick as a flash of lightning, his paw shot out and swiped at Cat's head. It was not a hard swipe, but it hurt.

'OW!' she yelled furiously. Without thinking, she flung out her right paw and gave Pokesley a mighty sock on the jaw.

Pokesley let out a terrible scream, which sounded like someone dragging their nails across a blackboard. He dashed back to the middle of the lawn, knocking Cat aside on the way, and began darting round in circles, screaming his cowardly head off. 'Help! Help! Save me!'

Cat was breathless and slightly giddy from the smack on the head. She braced herself for an invasion of angry Stinkwater cats. But before that could happen, the back door of the house opened. The nice young dental nurse ran into the garden.

'Hamish, you poor little darling!' she cried. 'Did that horrid cat attack you?'

Pokesley stopped screaming and started mewing pathetically. The dental nurse swept him up into her arms and kissed the top of his head. 'It's all right, I'll take care of you,' she soothed. She frowned down at Cat. 'SHOO!'

'Yes, SHOO!' Pokesley said smugly, over the crook of her arm. 'And don't come back. Tell my father that when Darson's the King, he'll have to call me SIR. And then we'll see who's a PLAPP!'

The dental nurse carried Pokesley into the house. Cat saw her through the window, giving the spoilt cat a Meaty Stick.

What a wimp, Cat thought scornfully.

She had not found the Blessed Sardine, but she was sure Pokesley knew more than he had told her. She decided to ask Biffy about Major Mincible. First, however, she must change back into a human – before the receptionist noticed she wasn't in the waiting room. Climbing back up to the spare bedroom was harder work than climbing down, and Cat's paws ached with the effort of clinging to the drainpipe. She squeezed herself through the open window. The Professor's alabaster stone was exactly where she had left it, in the middle of the bed. Cat flung herself on top of it. Moments later, she was a human girl again. She looked on the floor for her clothes.

Her clothes were not there.

Cat's heart swooped with panic. Heaven help her, she was NUDE AT THE DENTIST'S. This was just like being trapped in her worst nightmare, where she was nude in school assembly – only this time it was real. *Where were her clothes?*

Downstairs, she heard the receptionist calling. 'Catherine Williams!'

Aaagh! THINK!

It was chilly in the spare bedroom. Cat's naked body was covered with goose pimples. If they found her like this, she would DIE of embarrassment – and how could she possibly explain? This time, Mum would definitely think she had gone mad. She dragged the duvet off the bed, wrapped it round herself, and crept to the door. The landing was deserted. She could still hear the Hoover upstairs, but the drilling sound had stopped.

'Catherine Williams, please!'

On the other side of the landing the door to the MacWheesh bathroom stood slightly open. It would be more polite, Cat thought, to cover herself with a towel. She threw the duvet back on the bed and sprinted across to the bathroom. She was just about to grab a large yellow towel when she noticed something familiar hanging out of the laundry basket – one sleeve of her blue tracksuit.

'Oh, thank the Great Fish!' Cat muttered (not till afterwards did she wonder why she had thanked a Great Fish). Someone had put her clothes in the wash, and her trainers were under the sink. Feverish with the relief of it, Cat rescued her clothes from the laundry basket (yuk, they were lying on top of one of Mr MacWheesh's vests). In a matter of seconds she was fully dressed, with the alabaster stone lying safely in her pocket. She hurtled downstairs.

'Catherine?' The receptionist was in the waiting room, looking puzzled. For once, Cat did not blush puce when she told her lame story about 'getting lost'.

'In you go, then,' the receptionist said, pushing Cat through the surgery door.

'Ah, Catherrrrine!' There was Mr MacWheesh, with his white coat, rubber gloves and distressingly hairy nose. There, too, was the nice nurse, who had no idea that she had just told Cat to 'Shoo'.

Much later, when her parents thought she was asleep, Captain Girlcat made her report to Biffy.

'The whole day has been a failure,' she told him crossly. 'I haven't made friends with Darson's human, I haven't found out anything about the Sardine – and I had to have a filling!' The made-up cracked filling had turned out to be true. After all the tension of fighting Pokesley and hunting for her clothes, the human Cat had endured an injection, the drill and an unwanted close-up of the black hairs in Mr MacWheesh's nostrils. There had to be an easier way to find the Blessed Sardine.

Biffy told her about Major Mincible. 'Steer clear of him. He's Darson's right-paw cat. My spies tell me he's planning a raid this very night, at Fatoom Gutter.'

'A raid?' asked Cat. 'What does that mean?'

Biffy's wise old eyes were dark with foreboding. 'It means a BATTLE, and it's going to be tough. I'm taking in a paw-picked squad of my best cats. He'll never get that drain while I'm alive!'

Cat shivered. The way he spoke made the ends of her whiskers tingle. 'Let me come with you!'

'No, Captain,' Biffy said firmly. 'You must promise me to stay human, unless I give you a signal with the ringing ball. The Battle of Fatoom won't be a place for kittens!'

6
to the Country

Early next morning, before Cat was dressed and Mum had gone to work, Biffy limped in through the cat flap covered in blood.

'Biffy!' Cat gasped, flinging herself down on the floor beside him. 'What have they done to you?'

His left ear was badly torn. The left side of his striped face was plastered with dried blood and dirt. He collapsed on the kitchen floor. Cat gently stroked him, and he gave her hand a feeble lick. This, and the sorrowful expression in his eyes, told her that the Cockledusters had lost the Battle of Fatoom. How many other innocent cats had been wounded? She couldn't help bursting into tears.

Mum and Dad were very kind – they hated seeing their cat in pain just as much as Cat did. But they were a little puzzled that Cat was so upset.

'No, of course you don't need the day off school!'
Mum said. 'People don't take days off just because
their cat's been in a fight. Don't get in such a state,
darling – he'll be fine.' She took the brave, defeated
General to the vet on her way to work.

Cat spent a long, lonely day at school. Emily and
her gang pulled faces at her in the playground and
threw paper darts at her all through the afternoon
music lesson (Mr Martin only looked at the piano,
and you could get up to all sorts behind his back). For
once, Cat hardly noticed. She was too worried about
Biffy. Would he be all right? Had the Cockledusters
lost one battle or the whole war? Had the dying King
already been taken into slavery by the Stinkwaters?

She raced home, and found Biffy fast asleep in the
sitting room. Dad had made a special bed for him in
the best armchair. He lay upon his knitted blanket, his
rubber mice lined up beside him, one paw resting on
his ringing ball.

'The vet's stitched his ear, and he says the injections
will make him sleepy for a day or two,' Dad explained.
'But even though he's an old gentleman these days, the
vet reckons he's as fit as a fiddle.'

Biffy opened his eyes just a slit and unmistakably
smiled up at Cat. She hugged his neck, careful not to
hurt his war wound.

'Oh, Biffy – I'm so glad you're all right!'

'That's the second time you've called that cat

"Biffy", Dad said. 'Have you given him a new name? Should I fork out for a new collar-disc?'

'It's just a sort of nickname,' Cat said. She wished she could tell Dad the whole story – but how could she, without sounding completely barmy?

The rest of the afternoon and evening passed very quietly. Biffy snored wheezily in the armchair. Cat did geography homework and watched television. She ate supper with Mum and Dad, and went up to bed at the usual time.

To her surprise, Biffy's ringing ball was on the pillow. She had not seen him stir from the armchair – he must have managed to get upstairs while they were all eating. This must be another emergency, but she couldn't risk turning into a cat while her parents were awake. She set her alarm for one o'clock and drifted uneasily into sleep.

Cat wasn't normally very good at getting up. This time, however, she sat bolt upright in bed as soon as she heard the beep-beep-beep of her alarm clock. Perhaps being an occasional cat had given her some of a cat's alertness and readiness. Quickly, she grabbed the Professor's stone. She was getting used to the mysterious face filling her mind's eye, and the great rush of magic when she made her strange request for entry into the Temple of Pahnkh. The alabaster grew hot. Cattish energy surged into her shrinking limbs.

She was a cat.

Silently, Cat trotted out of her bedroom (she had left the door slightly open on purpose) and ran downstairs to meet Biffy.

Where was he? Cat thought she could pick his smell out of the tangle of smells, but she couldn't see him anywhere.

'Biffy?' she mewed softly. 'Here I am!'

There was no reply. Maybe he's waiting outside, Cat thought. Her tiny paws pattered noiselessly across the kitchen floor to the cat flap. She jumped through it into the dark garden. The night was full of sounds and scents, but there was still no sign of the General. Perhaps, in his wounded state, he had gone back to his armchair. Cat turned back towards the house.

Suddenly, she felt a heavy thump on her head, which made the whole world spin, and an agonizing pain in her face. Cat opened her mouth to shriek. A bony paw was clamped across it. She struggled and fought with all her strength, but escape was impossible. She was trapped. Giddy with pain and fear, Cat was hustled roughly through the shadows.

She had been tricked. Someone on the other side knew her secret, and the signal of the ringing ball. They had used it to catnap her – and now not a living soul, fur or flesh, knew where she was.

An evil female voice hissed in her ear, 'Sssstop wriggling – or we'll KILL you!'

There was a terrible smell of Stinkwater badness. Cat kept telling herself to be brave, but she had never felt less brave in her life. Where were they taking her? What did the Stinkwaters want with her? She felt herself being dragged across the road. She smelt the soil and dampness of a back garden. The catnappers pushed her through a door and threw her down upon a dirty, splintery wooden floor. Cat licked her lips and tasted blood.

'We got her,' said the evil female voice. 'The information was quite correct.'

'Well done, my dear. Well done, Major Mincible.' It was the flesh-creeping voice of Darson Stinkwater. They had brought her right into the heart of the enemy HQ – the back garden of Emily Baines.

Cat struggled into a sitting position. Using her human senses, she made out that she was in a greenhouse, stacked with flowerpots, spades, trays of seedlings and bags of peat. Darson Stinkwater was sitting on a large lawnmower. Beside him sat a white cat, with large splodges of black and light brown across her back.

'This is your future Queen,' Darson told Cat, 'Sleeza of Stinkwater, chief of my eight wives, and mother of my first two litters. Sleeza gave you that cut across your face – just to show you what her claws can do.'

Sleeza grinned at Cat and her claws gleamed like knives in the dim light. Cat recognized her. In the

 79

human world she was known as 'Tiny', and she lived at the Indian supermarket in Pole Crescent — Cat had seen her there countless times, sitting among the dusty bottles in the window.

A nasty tomcat voice snarled, 'Shall I KILL her now, Master?'

'Patience, Mincible,' said Darson. 'For the moment, this creature is more use to us ALIVE.'

Cat was desperately trying to think. When she had caught Pokesley scrabbling in the earth, she had seen him with a ringing ball and assumed he was burying it. But he must have been digging it up, ready to trick her. How did the Stinkwaters know about Biffy's secret signal? How did they know about her being a human? The Cockleduster cats had all been sworn to secrecy, yet one of them had betrayed her. This was a fearful, sickening thought.

'We've met already,' Darson said. 'You may bow to your King, girlcat.'

Through her terror, Cat was angry. 'You're not my King!'

'Let me interrogate her, Master!' hissed the tomcat.

Major Mincible was a very handsome cat, with beautiful black and silver markings, but the expression on his face made Cat shudder. His fangs gleamed as he leered at her.

'All in good time, Mincible,' said Darson, chuckling. 'First you must take the message to the Cockledusters.

Tell them we've got the human thing. If they want to see her alive again, they'd better send back Vartha!' He glared down at Cat. 'This is WAR, human thing. Last night, during the battle, the Cockledusters STOLE our daughter Vartha!'

'They didn't!' Cat cried. 'They'd never do a mean thing like that! Her poor humans would think she was lost!'

There was an unpleasant sound of Stinkwater laughter.

'She's sorry for the humans!' sniggered Sleeza. 'As if we cared about the big sillies who get our food. When you're at war, human thing, you can't afford to be sentimental about the SERVANTS!'

'Let me explain,' said Major Mincible. 'Vartha is Darson's oldest daughter and chosen one. When he has gone to the country, she will be the next Stinkwater leader. And she's going to marry ME – it's all arranged. So if Larfing Silex doesn't send her home immediately, we'll be sending you home instead – DEAD!'

'You'll never be human again,' hissed Darson. 'You'll be nothing but a little dead cat. They'll throw you away like a piece of rubbish!'

Cat swallowed hard several times. Her throat ached to break into the mews that were the cat version of crying, but she was determined not to let the Cockledusters down by showing her fear and despair.

'You'll never get away with this,' she said breath-lessly. 'If – if anything happens to me, General Biffy's regiment will destroy you all!'

'Oh no they won't!' snapped Sleeza. 'Because we'll have the power of the Sardine behind us. And when we have that, the whole kingdom will be ours!'

'Hang on,' Cat said, slowly. 'What do you mean, WHEN you have it? Don't you have the Sardine now?'

Darson's narrow face was suddenly hideous with rage. 'SSSSILENCE!' he hissed. 'It is ours, and that is all you need to know!'

'And the drains and gutters of Fatoom are ours already,' said Major Mincible. 'Did your baggy old General mention that I was the one who bit his ear? You can tell him he tasted AWFUL – if you ever see him again!'

'Lock her up!' ordered Darson.

Sleeza and Mincible pushed Cat into a huge flower-pot that was lying on its side. They turned it upside down, and Cat was trapped in a mouldy terracotta prison. The bottom of the flowerpot was her ceiling, and the little hole above showed a disc of slightly paler darkness. Otherwise, everything was black. With her needle-sharp cat's ears, Cat heard Sleeza, Darson and Mincible leaving the greenhouse. She was alone.

She collapsed in a trembling heap on the rough floor, and broke into miaows of utter desolation.

Nobody knew where she was. The Stinkwaters would claw her to death. Her poor parents would never know what had happened to her. She would never have a chance to tell them how much she loved them. The human part of her wept, and the cattish part mewed, until eventually she fell asleep.

She woke to the sound of her name, whispered urgently over and over again. 'Girlcat! Girlcat Verripritty! Can you hear me?'

Cat's head was foggy with sleep, fear and pain – the cut on her face throbbed horribly. It took her a few moments to recognize the voice of the cat from next door, Mrs Queenie Eatsmuch. Her heart gave a great leap of hope. 'Yes, I'm here!' she whispered. 'I can't get out – the flowerpot's too heavy!'

'Listen carefully,' whispered Mrs Eatsmuch. 'We're right in the heart of the Stinkwater camp, dear. This is Darson's land, and while we're here our lives aren't worth a Meaty Stick. Do as I tell you, keep quiet as a fish, and stay close!'

'How did you know I was here?'

'I saw the whole thing, dear,' whispered Mrs Eatsmuch. 'When Sleeza and Mincible catnapped you, I followed them. I waited till Mincible had gone off with his message.'

'And is it true?' Cat asked. 'Have you really stolen Darson's chief daughter?'

Mrs Eatsmuch sniffed scornfully. 'Certainly not! Don't listen to those Stinkwater LIES!'

'But Darson and Sleeza really think she's been cat-napped!'

'Maybe she ran away because she couldn't stand belonging to that horrid family,' suggested Mrs Eatsmuch.

'I'm so glad it wasn't anything to do with our side,' Cat said, very relieved. 'I know how it feels to be a prisoner now. Thanks for helping me.'

'Don't thank me yet, dear,' Mrs Eatsmuch said briskly. 'We're in a lot of danger here. I'm going to start shoving your prison towards the door. You can shove from the inside, and move it along the floor with your back legs. Do you understand?'

'Yes!'

'One – two – three – SHOVE!'

Both cats shoved at the flowerpot with all their strength. At last it began to move very slowly across the floor. The next shove took the flowerpot over the very edge of the doorstep. There was just enough space on the floor of her prison cell for Cat to slither out on to the garden path. She was free. Blissfully, she filled her small cat lungs with the fresh night air.

Mrs Eatsmuch sniffed busily. She swivelled her pointed brown ears to catch the sounds of the Stinkwater HQ. Everything was quiet, but the stench of danger was very strong. Though Cat couldn't have described the smell of danger as a human, she knew it perfectly when she was a cat – tingling, electric, bitter, it made her heart gallop in her little orange chest.

'Get under the hedge,' whispered Mrs Eatsmuch, 'and stick as close to me as you can!'

She made a sudden dive under the box hedge. Cat followed her. There was only a small space between the bottom of the hedge and the hard earth. The two cats had to crouch low, making themselves as long and thin as snakes.

'We have to get across the Wastes of Tidebolt,' Mrs Eatsmuch said over her shoulder. 'Then we'll be back in safe Cockleduster land. If we get separated and you meet our patrol, the password is "Sneezer" – do you understand, dear?'

'Yes, Mrs Eatsmuch.' Cat knew that the Wastes of Tidebolt meant the strip of road between the pavements – a shadowy no-cat's-land that marked the border between Cockleduster and Stinkwater. She tried not to sound as terrified as she felt.

Mrs Eatsmuch led them out of the hedge. They crept on to the path to the front gate.

'SSSTOPP!' A shape rocketed towards them from the top of a dustbin, and landed on the path in front of them.

Mrs Eatsmuch gave a little gasp of horror. It was Sleeza, every hair of her standing on end, as if she had her tail stuck in an electric socket.

 85

'Stand aside, Mrs Queenie Eatsmuch! The human thing belongs to ME!'

'I'm not afraid of you, Mrs Sleeza of Stinkwater,' Mrs Eatsmuch said calmly. 'You're nothing but a TUMFRIT!'

'Tumfrit' was cattish for 'coward and weakling', and a great insult. Cat was amazed that Mrs Eatsmuch dared to say such a thing to the wife of Darson Stinkwater.

'Tumfrit yourself, you old DROOPAG!*'' hissed Sleeza. 'Give me the human thing – or I'll make you sorry!'

'You know I can't let you have her,' Mrs Eatsmuch said. 'A human can't be harmed. It goes against all the laws of the Sardine – and the cat who breaks those laws is doomed!'

Sleeza let out a horrible, grating laugh. 'We make the laws now. The Sardine obeys us! It is our servant, and we own its power!'

Mrs Eatsmuch shuddered – Cat could see that she was deeply shocked by the wicked way Sleeza spoke of the Blessed Sardine. Keeping her green eyes pinned on Sleeza, Mrs Eatsmuch said quietly, 'Girlcat, will you be very brave and do exactly as I tell you?'

'Y-yes Mrs Eatsmuch,' gulped Cat.

'Don't worry, dear – I won't let Sleeza get her filthy paws on you.'

*Droopag - A foolish elderly female

Sleeza let out a long yowl of fury. 'Have it your own way, Droopag!'

'Run!' Mrs Eatsmuch muttered to Cat. 'Run for your life – don't stop till you get to the border!'

Cat burst into tears. She hated leaving the noble old lady alone with Sleeza – but Mrs Eatsmuch had given the order in the kind of voice your parents use when there is a real emergency, and Cat did not dare to disobey. She dashed through the front gate, across the enemy pavement and into the bleak Wastes of Tidebolt. Behind her, she heard an eerie scream from Sleeza, and a muffled cry of pain from Mrs Eatsmuch. She had to get help – the old lady cat was no match for the wife of Darson. Sobbing and trembling, Cat jumped to the safety of Cockleduster land.

Immediately, she was surrounded by cats. A familiar voice cried, 'Great Gills and Scales! You're safe!'

It was Biffy. His voice was weak and his legs were unsteady, but his old spirit gleamed in his eyes, and his wounded ear made him look even more of a tough fighting tom.

'She's SAFE!' Biffy called to the other cats. 'Call off the search party!'

Larfing Silex ran along the top of the wall, and jumped down to Cat's side. 'We got Darson's message – we were just going to look for you. Well, what a relief. Come here and I'll lick that cut on your face.'

'Never mind me – you've got to save Mrs

Eatsmuch,' Cat said urgently. 'She helped me to escape, and now she's in the enemy camp, and Sleeza's attacking her – oh, please do something!'

Biffy frowned. 'I'll take a paw-picked squad of our top fighters.' He raised his voice. 'Tuggard Steggings! The Donk Brothers! Elixa Atlas!' One by one, the sleek shapes of these cats flitted out of the shadows and lined up beside the gutter. They were all tough cats, famed for their fighting skills (Elixa Atlas, a young neutered female, was notorious even among the humans – most people in Tunnock Avenue had been scratched by 'Flossie' at Number 22).

Cat tried to join the fighters, but Biffy sternly head-butted her back to the garden gate.

'Not you, Captain – it's far too dangerous now the enemy knows you're human. Wait here.'

As silently as shadows, Biffy and the fighting cats streaked across the Wastes of Tidebolt, and into enemy land. Cat was glad to be left behind. She didn't think she was strong enough to tackle a cat like Sleeza, and the cut on her face was throbbing painfully. For what seemed like ages, but was actually about ten minutes, she waited in a fever of anxiety. Fearful sounds of battle drifted to her from across the Wastes – more Stinkwaters had rushed to help Sleeza, and the air was filled with snarls and screams.

Then the sounds stopped and an eerie silence fell.

Out in the Wastes, Cat saw a strange dark shape moving slowly towards her. She ran to the gutter. It was Biffy and his fighters, all squashed together in a furry mass. Their backs made a bed for the still body of Mrs Queenie Eatsmuch.

'Mrs Eatsmuch!' gasped Cat. 'What happened? Are you all right?'

The cats gently laid Mrs Eatsmuch on the small patch of lawn in Lucy's front garden. Elixa Atlas lapped up some muddy rainwater and dribbled it into Mrs Eatsmuch's mouth. The old cat was covered in blood. One of her front paws was smashed and there was a great slash across her belly.

'Hold on, Queenie,' Biffy said. 'My girlcat will wake the humans, and they'll take you to the Healing Place with the Pointed Sticks.'

But Queenie opened her eyes and held out her wounded paw. 'No, Nigmo,' she whispered painfully. 'No pointed stick can help me now – I shall soon be in the country.'

'Oh, Mrs Eatsmuch,' Cat blurted out desperately. 'Please let me try! I'll ring the vet's emergency number myself! I'll wake my mum!'

'No – too late –' gasped Mrs Eatsmuch. 'Just take my love to my little human girl—'

She sighed. A great shiver ran through her body, then a look of calm settled on her furry, bloodstained face. There was a long silence.

Elixa Atlas said, 'She's through the gate at the end of the long lane. That's how you get to the country.'

'No!' Cat cried. She burst into mews of sorrow. The brave old cat was dead, and it was all her fault.

Biffy's voice came out in a very wobbly mew, though he tried to keep it steady. 'By the Sardine, I'll miss her,' he said huskily. 'Best wife I ever had!' He made a growling, coughing sound, as if clearing his throat. 'Pay attention, cats. There will be a Grand Sending-Shout for Queenie Eatsmuch in my land tomorrow. Pass the word to every Cockleduster – we're going to give her a real HERO'S SHOUT!'

Cat was mewing her heart out, but she managed to hear about the Sending-Shout and understood that it was a cats' funeral service.

'Come along,' Biffy said to her. 'The sun will be back soon. You must change into a human.'

'What about her body?' Cat asked. 'You can't just leave it here!'

'She's not in it any more,' Biffy pointed out. 'And she doesn't need it now she's in the country.'

Cat was too exhausted and too sad to argue. She followed Biffy through his cat flap, back to the safety of their own kitchen.

'Remember,' he said, 'don't leave this land when you're a cat, unless I'm with you. I will wake you in tomorrow's dark and escort you to poor Queenie's Sending-Shout.'

'It was all my fault, Biffy,' Cat said. 'I was stupid to walk into Darson's trap!'

'Don't blame yourself,' Biffy said, in a very kind voice. 'How were you to know the ringing ball was a trick?' He frowned. 'Come to think of it, I'd better change my signal. Instead of the ringing ball, I'll leave my third-best squeaky mouse. Got that?'

'Yes, I've got it.' Cat was thinking hard. 'I wish I knew who told the Stinkwaters about me being human. And how did they find out about our signal?'

'We'll find the traitor,' Biffy said grimly. 'In the meantime, we'll keep the new signal a total secret – just between you and me. Got that?'

'Yes, Biffy.'

He licked her face. 'Don't be too sad about Queenie. The country's a wonderful place. She'll be as happy as a toad in a hole.'

'You don't know that,' muttered Cat, sobbing again.

'Well, I don't KNOW, exactly,' Biffy said thoughtfully. 'But it MUST be a wonderful place – nobody ever comes back from it, do they?'

He seemed to think this settled the question. Cat wished she could be as sure.

'Have a good rest, Biffy,' she said. 'I hope your ear feels better tomorrow.'

'And I hope your face feels better. Goodnight, dear Girlcat.'

Biffy went back to his invalid's armchair. Cat went to her bedroom, changed back into a human, and cried herself to sleep thinking of the brave old cat who had gone to the country to save her.

7
two SHouts

When Cat saw her face in the bathroom mirror next morning, she groaned aloud. How was she going to explain this? A huge red cut zig-zagged across her face, slicing through one eyebrow and the bridge of her nose. It was the cut Sleeza had given her with the steely tip of a lethal claw. It didn't hurt any more (it had stretched while Cat was turning back into a human), but it was still extremely visible. She tried disguising it with Mum's make-up, but that made it look worse. In the end, she went downstairs with a feeble story about cutting her face on a sharp drawer-handle.

Mum was suspicious — when had this happened? Where was the blood? — but she had to rush off to work. Luckily, Dad did not have such a suspicious

 93

nature and he was only sympathetic. He said Cat was a 'poor sausage', and even offered her the day off school.

Oh, the misery, injustice and sorrow of it – a once-in-a-lifetime offer and she had to turn it down. 'Thanks, but I'd rather go in today,' she lied. 'There's stuff I have to do.'

Cat had no idea how she was going to manage it, but she had to give Mrs Eatsmuch's dying message to Lucy. There was no sign of Lucy in the street – as usual, she had bolted off to school ahead of Cat. In the front garden of the house next door, however, Cat saw Lucy's mother. Mrs Church (small and shy, like Lucy) was digging in the flowerbed with a shovel. A black plastic binbag lay on the lawn beside her. Every few moments she stopped digging to wipe her eyes.

Cat's own eyes blurred with tears. This was awful. The binbag was the coffin of poor Queenie Eatsmuch, and Mrs Church was digging her lonely grave. Never again would they see Mrs Eatsmuch's comfortable form strolling along the top of the garden wall. No more would she wash her face on the front doorstep. The whole Cockleduster side of Tunnock Avenue seemed empty without her, and Cat was sure the cats she passed looked unusually mournful. She was nearly late for school because she met Shouter Prendergast outside the pub. The stout black-and-white cat rubbed himself against Cat's legs. She bent down to stroke him, and he nuzzled her hand with his face – purring all the time, his sympathy bridged the gulf between cat and human. He rolled over on his back, and Cat gratefully tickled his enormous white belly. Kind old thing, he was doing his best to cheer her up.

If only there had been a way of cheering up Lucy. She sat in class as silent and self-contained as ever, but her eyes were red and puffy. Cat's heart ached for her. This was no time to be shy, she decided. There had to be a way of giving Lucy just a little hint of the truth, so she would know her cat had died a heroine.

She cornered Lucy beside the drinking fountains at morning break. 'Hi.'

Lucy jumped like a startled fawn. 'Oh – hi.'

'I just wanted to say – I heard about your cat, and – and I'm really sorry.'

'Thanks,' Lucy whispered. She hung her head. There was a silence.

'She was a lovely person – I mean, animal,' offered Cat.

'Thanks,' Lucy whispered again.

'I know how sad you are,' Cat blurted out eagerly, desperate to console. 'But you should be very proud of Quee – I mean Puss-Pie. She died to save someone's life. And she didn't suffer too much. She passed away peacefully, in the arms of her first husband.'

Cat stopped suddenly, and felt a blush surging into

her face. She had said far too much, and ended up babbling all the sentences that had been circling in her head all night. Lucy was staring at her as if she had gone crazy.

'I only wanted to say how brave she was. And how kind she was to me.'

'What are you talking about?' Lucy had gone very pale. She backed away from Cat. 'You're making fun of me!'

'Oh, no!'

'I think you're very mean to make fun of me today,' Lucy said. 'Just leave me alone!'

She darted away. Cat was left feeling helpless and foolish. She had tried to cheer Lucy up, and as usual she had only made things worse – but she was all the more determined to give her Queenie's message. All through afternoon school she wondered how to do it. Should she send her a letter? No – it would all look even barmier written down. Perhaps she should ask Mum to invite Lucy and her mother round to supper? But suppose they refused to come?

Finally, when she was walking home from school, Cat made a great decision. Lucy deserved to hear Queenie's last words – but she would never believe it unless she knew the whole truth. Suddenly, Cat wanted Lucy to understand everything. For some reason, she trusted the shy girl next door. She was going to let her into the secret.

Cat turned into Tunnock Avenue. Lucy was just about to step through her front gate. Impulsively, Cat broke into a run. 'Lucy! Wait! Lucy!'

Lucy froze, with one hand on the gate and a look of astonishment on her pale face.

Cat raced to catch up with her. 'I'm not making fun of you,' she said breathlessly. 'You have to listen to me – I did it all wrong this morning—'

'Just leave me alone,' Lucy said. Her voice was weary. 'What's the point of hassling me like this? It can't be any fun.'

'I was only trying to tell you how much I loved your cat,' Cat said. 'You should be very proud of her.'

'Proud?' Now Lucy was bewildered. 'What on earth are you talking about? You didn't know my cat!'

'Look – I haven't gone mad, I'm not being mean, and I'm not making anything up,' Cat said. 'I have something very important to show you. Come to my bedroom.'

'What?'

Cat sighed impatiently. 'It's a total secret. You have to swear not to tell anyone. Ask your mum if you can have tea at my house.'

Lucy was still bewildered, and more than a little suspicious, but she was also beginning to be very curious. 'My mum's at work,' she said. 'Mrs Pecking upstairs sort of keeps an eye on me.'

'Then tell Mrs Pecking.' Cat was feverish with

 97

excitement. Suddenly, she had to reveal the secret before it exploded out of her like a firework. 'If you come to tea with me now, you'll never have to do it again – or even speak to me. Please!'

'Oh no, I don't think—'

'You've got to!' Cat cried. 'You think you'd be taking a risk, but I'm taking a much bigger one. I'll be giving you the power to get me into a lot of trouble – so you'd better not turn out to be a cow!'

There was a short silence. Lucy surprised Cat by suddenly grinning. 'I won't go and tell Emily Baines, if that's what you mean.'

Both girls relaxed into laughter. Somehow, the glass wall between them had finally cracked. They had taken the first important step into the state of Being Friends. All at once, Cat felt strong and optimistic. She waited at the gate while Lucy told Mrs Pecking upstairs that she was having tea next door. Then the two of them walked round to the back of Cat's house.

'My mum's out at work too,' Cat said. 'My dad works at home, so he's always there after school. Unless he's away digging.'

'That must be nice,' Lucy said. 'My parents are divorced. I don't see my dad much.' Her voice was calm, but Cat could feel the sadness underneath.

'Poor you.'

Lucy shrugged. 'I expect I'll get used to it.'

The back door was open. Dad was in the kitchen,

wearing a pink apron with a big red heart on the front, chopping onions.

'Hi, Dad.'

'Hi, Cat. How's that cut?'

'Fine. Can Lucy stay for tea?'

Dad smiled over his shoulder. 'Of course. Hi, Lucy.'

'We're going upstairs,' Cat said. 'We'll be in my bedroom, and we don't want to be disturbed – got that?'

'Yes, Madam,' Dad said. 'I'll call you when it's ready.'

Cat led Lucy up the stairs to her bedroom, wishing Lucy wouldn't walk so slowly. Lucy was very stiff and cautious and stood in the middle of the rug like a soldier at attention. Cat pulled down her bedroom blinds. She pushed the big wooden toybox against the door. 'I have to be careful,' she explained. 'I don't want my dad to charge in at the wrong moment. Sit on the bed – and please don't scream.'

Lucy sat down on the bed. 'Scream?'

'Some people might,' Cat said. 'I ought to warn you, this could be a bit of a shock.'

Her heart was hammering. Suppose the stone didn't work in front of another person, and Lucy thought she was insane? Worse – suppose Lucy fainted, or died of a heart attack?

There was no going back now. Cat pulled the Professor's stone out of her jewellery box. She embraced the piece of alabaster, and waited for the image of the strange black cat to swamp her mind.

Inside her head, she heard her own voice seeking admittance to the Temple. It took a little longer than usual, but gradually the black face and yellow eyes grew bigger, and the watchful face of Lucy began to stretch into a mask of absolute amazement.

Cat was a cat.

The small marmalade cat sneezed twice and scrabbled out of the warm heap of human clothes.

Lucy backed away across the duvet, but she did not scream. She simply stared and stared, until she seemed about to stare her eyes right out of her head. Cat let out a couple of mews. She trotted across the room and played with the blind-cord for a few minutes. She jumped gracefully on to the chest of drawers and promenaded up and down the rug. She wanted to take her time and do a few cattish things, so that Lucy would not think she had dreamed it all.

When she thought she had done enough, Cat sprang back on to the alabaster stone and rapidly changed back into a human. It was embarrassing to be nude in front of Lucy. She hurried back into her clothes.

Lucy's eyes were like saucers. She didn't say a word until Cat sat down on the bed beside her. Then she said, 'That — that wasn't some kind of trick, was it?'

'Come on!' protested Cat. 'I wouldn't know how to do a "trick" like that. You saw, didn't you? I'm a real cat. And you're the only other human in the world who knows!'

'Human? What do you mean?'

'The other cats know,' Cat said. 'That's how I met Puss-Pie. It was because of me that she died.'

And she launched into the whole mad story, from the arrival of the Professor's stone to last night's attempted catnapping. Lucy was a very good listener, who only interrupted to ask useful questions. The story took such a long time that the sunlight faded on the other side of the blind, and Dad called from downstairs that supper was ready.

'Just a second!' Cat called back. Her voice was croaky because she was crying. Lucy was also crying. They had reached the part about Queenie's dying message.

'So you see,' Cat said, 'she loved you very much, and her very last thoughts were about you. I thought you should know.'

'Thanks,' whispered Lucy.

'She's a national heroine.'

Lucy wiped her eyes with her sleeve. 'Thanks,' she whispered again.

'I – I saw your mother burying her this morning,' Cat said.

Lucy nodded. 'I didn't want to be there. I just put her catnip hedgehog in the binbag with her, gave her a kiss and went to school. The hedgehog was her favourite toy. I didn't want her to feel lonely.' The tears slid down her cheeks and made wet circles on the duvet cover.

Hesitantly, Cat reached out to take Lucy's hand. 'She won't be lonely in the country.'

'What country?'

'I don't know,' Cat admitted. 'It's where cats go when they die. Heaven, I suppose. I'm so very sorry about all this, Lucy. I know it was my fault.'

'You couldn't help it,' Lucy said. 'But I'm going to miss her so much. We've had her since I was a baby. I do so wish I'd had a chance to say goodbye.'

Cat had an idea. 'Maybe you'd feel better if you came to her funeral.'

'What funeral?'

'I don't mean a human funeral, with cars and flowers. The cats call it a Sending-Shout. You could stay the night here and come with me.'

For the first time, Lucy looked a little less sad. 'May I? Won't your parents mind?'

'Oh no. They're always begging me to have friends round.' Cat jumped off the bed, to push the toybox away from the door. 'Biffy will wake me for the Shout, and before I turn into a cat, I'll wake you.'

Cat only had to touch Lucy's shoulder once, and she woke immediately.

'It's time!' Cat whispered. 'Follow me. Be as quiet as

you can. Our back door is bolted at the top. You'll need to stand on a chair to unbolt it. Then you just turn the key.'

Lucy nodded, and wriggled out of her sleeping bag to put on her dressing gown. Her mother had called round after supper with Lucy's things – all the parents were startled that the two girls were suddenly such friends.

Professor Katzenberg's stone grew hot in Cat's hand. She felt the familiar tingling in her limbs and, in a matter of minutes, she was a cat.

Biffy was waiting on the landing. 'I'm not sure this is wise,' he grumbled. 'Can we trust this human?'

'Of course you can trust Lucy!' Cat said firmly. 'And think how Mrs Eatsmuch loved her.'

'Well, all right,' Biffy sighed. 'For Queenie's sake we'll allow your human into our Shout. But you'll have to look after her – I'll be sitting with the other husbands.'

'Goodness, how many husbands are there?'

'Just the five now,' Biffy said solemnly. 'Number Two got knocked down by a van and went ahead. Come along.'

The two cats and the human girl crept down the stairs to the darkened kitchen. Cat and Biffy jumped through the cat flap. Lucy pulled up a chair and unbolted the back door. Out in the garden Cat mewed at Lucy, in a way she hoped was reassuring. It was certainly a strange sight for a human. A long, silent

 103

file of local cats streamed across the lawn. Their bright eyes studded the night like stars. They gathered in a furry press around the compost heap. On top of the compost heap sat the Crown Prince and Princess, Larfing Silex and the Shouter Everlasting Prendergast.

Biffy joined a small group of elderly toms – Queenie's husbands. There was a large crowd of Queenie's children, grandchildren and great-grandchildren. Cat went to sit near Elixa Atlas, among the lady cats. She looked round for Lucy and saw her in the shadows, leaning against the trunk of the pear tree. None of the cats seemed to have noticed her. What a shame, Cat thought, that Lucy wouldn't be able to understand the ceremony. She decided to remember as many details as possible, so that she could tell Lucy afterwards.

'Cockledusters!' cried Princess Bing.

The silent cats bowed, in a great furry wave.

'Cockledusters, I thought our next Sending-Shout would be for my husband's father – but amazingly, the King is still alive.' There was a silence. 'You may cheer,' said the Princess coldly.

The husbands, Elixa Atlas and a few others purred loyally.

'We didn't imagine,' said Princess Bing, 'that poor Queenie Eatsmuch would get to the country before him. The King says he'll be happy to take any messages for Queenie when he goes.'

Elixa Atlas muttered, 'I'd like to ask her who got that lovely catnip hedgehog!'

'Shhhh!' hissed all the husbands.

'Well, Queenie doesn't need it any more,' said Elixa Atlas.

'Don't be greedy!' a female cat scolded. 'And anyway, she always said she wanted ME to have it!' (Cat decided not to tell Lucy about this bit.)

'Mrs Eatsmuch was a brave and noble cat,' the Princess went on. 'And we have gathered here to make her a great Shout, that will be heard in all the sunny sleeping-places of that beautiful country to which she has moved. But before that, the Reverend Everlasting Prendergast has another ceremony to Shout.'

Despite the sad occasion, the Crown Princess was sleek and satisfied, and altogether rather pleased with herself. 'I'm delighted to announce that a BRIDE has been found for my son, Prince Crasho!'

This piece of news caused a sensation among the cats in the audience.

'Well I never!' said Elixa Atlas. 'I thought she'd never get that useless Crasho off her paws!'

'Since we are in a state of war,' continued the Crown Princess, 'we will make the engagement-scratches now. Be quick about it, Prendergast,' she added, to the reverend.

Everlasting Prendergast gave the crowd one of his

kindly smiles. 'Yes, Your Highness. In the midst of sorrow, there is joy. Step forward, Prince Crasho!'

The young Prince scrambled up the compost heap. He looked as sulky as ever, and his mother gave him a quick smack on the head as he passed.

'Step forward, Ploshkina!'

Out of the shadows stepped a beautiful blue-grey cat, with slanted yellow eyes. She bowed gracefully to the Crown Prince and Princess.

'Very elegant!' whispered Elixa Atlas.

'This noble lady comes from a far kingdom,' shouted Everlasting Prendergast, 'and is related by thirty-six removes to the House of Cockleduster. The wedding will take place tomorrow. Now we will Shout their betrothal. Let the scratches be made!'

Prince Crasho was licking one of his paws. Princess Bing gave him a smart smack on the nose. 'Crasho! Get on with it!'

Still the young Prince hesitated. The human side of Cat thought he looked very miserable for someone about to be married. Very slowly, he went to the bottom of the compost heap and made two quick scratches in the earth with his left paw. Almost too quietly to hear, he muttered, 'I scratch.'

Some rude toms at the back shouted, 'Speak up! What's the point if we can't hear?'

Crown Prince Cockie raised his head. 'I did a very quiet scratch when I got engaged to Bing,' he said. 'My mother was crying so loudly that nobody heard anything at all. But it was still legal.'

The lovely Ploshkina jumped down to Prince Crasho's side. Her scratches were firm, and she made them with a flourish. 'I SCRATCH!' she announced loudly.

There was a burst of cattish cheering. Mackerella, daughter of Biffy, ran to the top of the compost heap. She threw back her tabby head and let out a long, wavering YOWWL. To Cat's human ear, the sound was agonizing. The cat part of her, however, thrilled to the sound of Mackerella's lovely voice, and the exquisite music she was screaming.

While she sang, the Reverend Everlasting Prendergast solemnly licked the whiskers of Prince Crasho and Ploshkina. The young couple bowed to Crasho's royal parents and sat down.

Now the most serious part of the meeting began. Mackerella's joyful wedding song changed to a lament:

'*OQueenieHowTerribleHelpYouAreDeadAndCoveredWith HugeDeepScratchesButThat'sOnlyYourBodyYourSoulRestsWith TheSardine . . .*'

'Bloody cats!' a human voice yelled across the back gardens. 'Shut up!' (Cat thought she recognized Mr Gibbs from Number 14.)

The cats did not understand this vulgar interruption, and ignored it.

'Let us raise a Mighty Shout!' cried Everlasting Prendergast. 'A Shout that will make the whole country tremble!'

Cat braced herself for more yowling, but the 'Shout' was not something the cats did with their voices. It was a low purr, too deep to hear clearly, that vibrated inside their heads. Cat felt the vibration inside her own head – she was joining in, without even realizing.

Over by the pear tree, Lucy was sitting on the ground, crying. Her sobs echoed in the silence.

'What is that?' demanded Princess Bing. 'And why is it making that AWFUL noise?'

'I call it RUDE,' said a sour lady cat.

'Is it eating something?' asked Prince Cockie.

It was probably the height of bad manners to interrupt a Sending-Shout, but Cat couldn't bear the Cockledusters to have the wrong idea about Lucy. 'No!' she blurted out. 'Sorry, Your Highness – but she's my friend, and she's not being rude.' Every furry face turned towards her. 'She was Mrs Eatsmuch's human,' she explained. 'The very one she sent her love to when she died. The noise she's making is called "crying" – it's what humans do when they – I mean, we – are very sad.'

The cats looked at each other, and at Lucy – who went on sobbing.

'Poor little human,' Elixa Atlas said kindly. 'Queenie

was ever so fond of her. I wish we could show her how sorry we are.'

In the human side of her brain, Cat had a brilliant idea. 'You can!' she cried. 'Anyone who wants to comfort my friend should lick her hand!'

Whispers ran through the crowd. 'Lick it? Why?'

'Perhaps she means it's dirty . . .'

'Do humans lick each other at their Sending-Shouts?'

Cat jumped up. 'Just watch me.' She ran through the crowd to Lucy's side. Lucy's hand lay in her lap. Cat gave it one lick. She stepped back, and the nearest cat took her place. One by one, every single cat – even the royal family – lined up beside Lucy to lick her hand with their sandpapery tongues.

Lucy stopped crying. She gazed at the cats in wonderment. There was no mistaking their sympathy. When her tears came back they were mixed with smiles, like the sun shining through rain.

'Oh, you darlings!' she murmured. 'You dear things! I'll do anything to help you save your Sardine.' She leaned forward and scooped Cat into her arms. 'I don't know if you can understand this – but thank you!'

8
SCANDAL

'I can't get over you two,' Dad said next morning. 'You don't say a word to each other for months – then all of a sudden, you can't stop talking.' He held two rucksacks over the breakfast table. 'If you don't get a move on, you'll be late for school – and Lucy's mother will never let her stay in this badly run household again.'

Cat and Lucy had been too busy talking to notice the time.

'Sorry, Dad.' Cat grabbed her rucksack. 'Is my recorder in there?'

'Yes, and so is Lucy's – her mother brought it round this morning.'

Lucy, who was still a little shy with Dad, said, 'Thanks for having me, Mr Williams.'

Dad said, 'It's been a great pleasure, Miss Church – and do please call me "Julian".'

Cat and Lucy hurried out of the house and along the road, talking furiously. Lucy wanted every single detail of the cat world, and bombarded Cat with questions about the Sending-Shout, the lost Sardine and the various cats of the Cockleduster Court.

'I hope you don't mind,' she said seriously, 'but I really do want to help – I can't bear to think of any more cats dying like Puss-Pie.'

'It's lovely having someone to tell,' Cat said. 'I was afraid you'd say it was all rather silly. You know – a war over a Sardine.'

'Two of the Stinkwaters nearly killed you,' Lucy said. 'There's nothing silly about that. You can't risk being alone as a cat until you've found the traitor.'

'Traitor? Do you mean Pokesley?'

'Not Pokesley.' Lucy was patient. 'You said yourself, he couldn't have known your secret. Some other cat betrayed you to the Stinkwaters – maybe a cat you think of as a friend.'

This was a disturbing idea – did one of those friendly, furry faces belong to a traitor?

'It's such a shame the Professor's stone doesn't work for you,' Cat sighed. 'You're so clever – I bet if you could turn into a cat you'd know all the right questions to ask, just like a detective in a film.'

They had tried turning Lucy into a girlcat that

morning, and were both very disappointed to find that the magic only seemed to work on Cat. Lucy would have loved to speak the cat language and Cat would have loved a girlcat companion, but it couldn't be helped.

'Never mind,' Lucy said. 'There's still plenty I can do. I'll apply my cool, analytical mind to the detective work, while you deal with the cat side of things. OK?'

'OK. I think . . .' Cat halted just outside the school gates. Her face was hot. 'I think we make a pretty good team, don't you?'

Lucy smiled. 'I think Mrs Queenie Eatsmuch would be proud of us.'

Biffy woke Cat at half past midnight, and would not stop butting her with his head until she had stumbled out of bed and changed herself into a cat.

'What are you doing?' she demanded sleepily, as soon as she could speak cattish. 'Don't you remember? You told me not to come to the royal wedding because it was too risky turning into a cat again!'

Biffy's green eyes were tragic. 'There isn't go to be any wedding,' he said. 'It's all over, and the House of Cockleduster is covered in SHAME!'

Cat yawned. 'Why? What's happened?'

'Prince Crasho has run off with Vartha Stinkwater!'

'What?'

'They've ELOPED, that's what,' Biffy said. 'It seems

that when Vartha ran away from home, she hid in the shed-place in Crasho's land. The young PLAPP says he's in love with her!'

Both the cattish and human sides of Cat couldn't help thinking this was rather romantic. 'You can't blame them for falling in love!'

Biffy was shocked. 'A Cockleduster Prince can't go round falling in love with Stinkwaters!'

'Why not?'

'Because . . . because . . .' Biffy couldn't think of a reply. 'Because IT'S JUST NOT DONE!'

'I'm not surprised Crasho and Vartha ran away, if everyone's being so mean to them,' Cat said. 'Does anyone know where they might be hiding?'

'No,' sniffed Biffy. 'They left a message with the dog who lives with Larfing Silex, and they haven't been seen since. Our Prince, and the daughter of our worst enemy! It's a disgrace!'

Cat yawned again – her adventures over the past few nights had made her terribly tired. 'I don't see what I'm supposed to do about it. What do you need me for?'

'Oh, you haven't heard the half of it,' the old General said darkly. 'That young Plapp has jumped straight into the paws of Darson Stinkwater. Come along – emergency meeting at the palace – at the double!'

The 'palace' was the Watsons' house, home of the

 113

dying King Cockleduster the Ninth. When Cat and Biffy climbed through the cat flap, they found the place in uproar. Through an open door Cat could hear sounds of distant human voices, and loud human snores. Old Mr Watson had fallen asleep in front of the television in the sitting room. None of the cats took the slightest notice of him.

The fat old King dozed in his basket. Princess Bing and Ploshkina were both crying. Prince Cockie sat sullenly beside his dying father. Larfing Silex kept repeating, 'Oh, dear! Oh dear!' Only the Reverend Everlasting Prendergast was keeping calm.

He bowed to the weeping, spitting Princess Bing. 'Your Highness, the girlcat is here.'

'She's heard about our SHAME!' wailed Princess Bing. 'But soon the WHOLE WORLD will know! Oh, when I get my paws on that boy! How DARE he fall in love with that — that little SCARLAP*? Oh, this will KILL Father!'

'No it won't,' Prince Cockie said bitterly. 'Nothing kills Father. Look at him — sound asleep, while we're all worrying ourselves into the country!'

The Princess ignored him. She looked at Cat. 'Greetings, human thing.'

Cat bowed. 'Greetings, Your Royal Highness.'

'We need your human help once again. Shouter Prendergast, tell her about the message.'

*Scarlap — An unscrupulous young female

The saintly Sardine-Shouter was very solemn. 'I've had a message from Darson Stinkwater. He says he's got Crasho – and if we want to see him alive again, we have to pay a ransom. But we can't do it without you.'

Cat didn't understand. 'Why not? I don't know anything about cat money.'

'Money? What's that?' asked Shouter Prendergast. 'The ransom the Stinkwaters have demanded is a tin of tuna – in OIL, not BRINE. They want it opened and left at Woshnab Point.' (Cat understood that this meant the alley round the back of the Admiral Tunnock.) 'We have until Saturday night. If they don't get the tuna, they say they'll send Crasho home IN PIECES!'

Biffy was seething with anger. 'The CHEEK of it! Already planning their victory feast! Your Highness, let me lead a raid on his back garden!'

'Peace, Biffy!' cried Shouter Prendergast. 'Must more lives be lost?'

Cat was alarmed by the warlike glint in Biffy's eyes, and the snarl in his voice. She could not allow him to be hurt again. 'I can easily get the tuna,' she said. 'Don't worry, Biffy – it'll be quite safe. I won't have to turn myself into a cat this time. The Stinkwaters can't do anything to me while I'm a human.'

Everlasting Prendergast gave Cat's paw a friendly lick. 'Sensible human, when all around you are distracted by the hiccups of sorrow. You're quite right, all you have to do is open the tin of tuna (in oil, not brine), and leave it in the agreed place at Woshnab Point. It's near my land, so I'll be taking it from there.'

'Won't that be dangerous?' Cat asked. 'Why don't you let me do everything?'

The Shouter smiled. 'You're a brave young thing – but I must be left alone. Darson said the tuna has to be delivered by ONE CAT – no other cats OR humans. And as a Sardine-Shouter, I shall be under the protection of the Great Fish. Even Darson would never harm a Shouter.'

A cattish murmur of admiration ran through the room. How brave the Reverend was, Cat thought. How great was his faith in the Blessed Sardine!

'Bless you, Prendergast,' sniffed Princess Bing. 'May the Slimy Bits guide thee.'

('"Goodbye,' muttered the other cats solemnly.)

There was a loud human 'HRRUMPH!' from the next room. Instantly, all the cats became as still and silent as statues. They heard Mr Watson struggling out of his armchair, yawning noisily and switching off the television. Biffy jumped through the cat flap and held it open for the others. One by one, the cats seemed to melt through it like shadows. By the time Mr Watson shuffled into his kitchen, the dying King was the only cat left in the house.

Peeping through the flap, Cat saw Mr Watson bend down over the King's basket. He stroked the old cat's pointed brown ears, and Cat heard him murmuring, 'Dear old boy!'

She thought about the thousands of years of friendship between cats and humans, and wondered if the cats knew how deeply they were loved.

'According to Bing,' Cat said, 'it's all an evil Stinkwater plot. She says Vartha made Crasho fall in love with her, then lured him into the enemy camp. But what would be the point of that? Crasho wouldn't be much use to Darson. He's not really much use to any-one.'

'And this sudden demand for tuna seems a bit strange,' Lucy said. She was at Cat's house having tea, so Cat could describe the emergency meeting and the scandalous elopement – there hadn't been a chance at school.

'It's not strange if you're a cat,' Cat pointed out. 'When I'm a cat, I find tuna totally delicious. And it's very difficult to get at because cats can't open tins.'

Lucy was frowning thoughtfully. 'Who carried the message about the ransom?'

'Everlasting Prendergast,' Cat said. 'You know – Widnes from the pub. He's such a darling.'

'It just seems an odd thing for Darson to do. Did anyone else know about it? Or do you just have Prendergast's word?'

'Hang on,' Cat said. She stopped eating. 'Are you saying the Reverend's the traitor? No, that's impossible!'

'Why?' Lucy asked coolly. 'It makes a lot of sense! Old Everlasting could have told your secret to the Stinkwaters. Come to that, he could have told them where the Blessed Sardine was hidden – nobody knows for sure that it was Pokesley. And he'd be in a perfect position to steal it. I think you should watch that Sardine-Shouter of yours.'

Cat giggled. 'Don't be silly. He's just an old softy – he says sorry to flies when he eats them. It couldn't possibly be him! It would be like Friar Tuck betraying Robin Hood to the Sheriff of Nottingham.'

'All the same,' Lucy said, with a surprising amount of determination in her gentle voice, 'I think you'll find I'm right.'

On Saturday morning, Cat took Biffy to the vet's to have the stitches taken out of his ear. He sat sleepily in his pet-carrier. Cat put it on the floor and sat down on one of the plastic chairs in the waiting room. She liked the waiting room at the vet's – it was fascinating to see people with their animals. Today, there was one lady with a rather smelly old rabbit, and Marcus Snow from the pub. At Marcus's feet was a large wicker pet-carrier containing the Reverend Everlasting Prendergast.

Cat and Marcus were in the same class at school. He was a thin, quiet, dark-haired boy.

'Hi,' said Cat.

'Hi,' said Marcus. 'What's up with your cat?'

'He was in a fight a few nights ago. He had stitches in his ear. What's up with poor old Widnes?'

Marcus laughed. 'Don't feel too sorry for him – the vet says his main problem is greed. He's got arthritis because he's so fat. And he's so fat because he can't stop eating. The vet put him on a strict diet, and now he's trying to find out why the diet isn't working.'

Cat stroked Shouter Prendergast's stubby paw through the bars of his carrier. 'Poor old thing, I bet he hates being on a diet.'

'He certainly does,' Marcus said, grinning – he seemed rather proud of his greedy, diet-proof cat. 'He tries to nick food off our plates. My dad's put up notices in the pub, telling the customers not to feed him. And he keeps on getting fatter. My dad says he must be getting food by blackmailing other cats!'

Cat managed to laugh, but her heart swooped. *Blackmailing other cats!* Or maybe kidnapping other cats and threatening to kill them! Only a very greedy cat would be prepared to kill for a tin of tuna – a very greedy cat on a strict diet. It was shocking, but it all fitted. Cat remembered now how the Reverend Prendergast had been so particular about tuna 'in oil, not brine'. It looked as if Lucy had been right.

'Widnes!' called the nurse.

Marcus smiled at Cat and hefted his heavy pet-carrier into the surgery. He had no idea that his cuddly old pet was a master criminal, almost certainly spying for the Stinkwaters. Cat looked down at Biffy's white-and-tabby face, which was squashed against the front of his carrier. Poor old Biffy, he thought the world of Everlasting Prendergast. This was going to be a dreadful shock.

9
SPYING

'It's ridiculous! It's nonsensical! It's just plain WICKED!' thundered Biffy. 'I'll have you know, young Madam, that in MY day, kittens had more respect for their elders and betters! How DARE you insult Shouter Prendergast?'

'He could be a master criminal!' argued Cat. She had not expected this to be such hard work. She had taken the risk of turning herself into a cat as soon as she got home – but Biffy refused to hear a word against the oily Shouter. She had never seen him so angry. 'Look,' she said, 'I'm not saying there's any proof – but you must admit, it all fits. And it would explain who told the Stinkwaters about me being a human.'

'That's enough, Captain! The Shouter is NOT a spy – it's outrageous!'

'Prove me wrong, then,' Cat said boldly. 'When I deliver the tuna, send in someone like Elixa Atlas to see what he does with it. I bet you any number of Meaty Sticks he eats it all himself!'

'Elixa Atlas? I'm supposed to spare one of my best fighters for some WOODLE-FOODLE damn silly idea? Certainly NOT!'

And that was obviously Biffy's last word. Cat hated quarrelling with her cat, but she could not afford to waste any time – not when furry lives might be in danger. Sighing, she turned herself back into a human, put on her clothes and called Lucy. Lucy was guarding the bedroom door in case Mum or Dad came upstairs. She wrenched the door open eagerly. 'Well?'

'It's hopeless,' Cat said crossly. 'He says it's all a pack of wicked lies, and it flies in the face of the Sardine to spy on a Shouter.'

Both girls watched Biffy. He scratched one ear with his back leg and stalked out of the room, in an offended way.

Lucy said, 'Even I can see he's angry. We'd better not make any plans until he's out of earshot.'

'It's all right,' Cat said. 'We can say anything we like in front of Biffy – he can't understand human language.'

'None at all? Not even a word here and there?' Despite the emergency, Lucy could not help being interested.

'They can usually recognize the noise their name makes,' Cat said. 'Otherwise, human speech is as strange to them as the cat language is to us.'

'Can you understand humans when you're a cat?'

'Yes,' Cat said. 'Though it sounds a bit muzzy. But I can't understand cats when I'm a human.'

'That's a shame,' Lucy said. 'It'd be far easier to spy on Prendergast if you had the language.'

Cat frowned. 'He's made sure there won't be any cats near him. He demanded tuna because he knows only a human can deliver it. And he knows I can't risk being captured again, so there's absolutely no chance that I'll turn up as a cat — Lucy!' With a surge of excitement, Cat suddenly saw what had to be done. 'That's it! YOU can deliver the tuna, and I can follow Prendergast AS A CAT! It's the last thing he'll expect!'

'What?' Lucy was startled. 'Don't be silly!'

'It's not silly, it's perfect!'

'For one thing,' Lucy said, 'Prendergast will see that I'm not you.'

'I don't think he'll notice,' Cat said. 'Cats aren't very good at telling humans apart. And the reek of tuna will cover your smell — he won't suspect a thing.'

Lucy shook her head. 'I can't let you do it, Cat. It's too risky. Suppose the Stinkwaters caught you again?'

'Don't you see? I'll have you with me as a human guard!' Cat was delighted with her own genius, and burning to start her spying mission. 'If I'm in danger I'll mew for you, and you can save me.'

'What if they cover your mouth?'

Cat was impatient. 'If I go quiet for too long, you can come and look for me. Come on, Lucy! I know we can do it!'

'You have to promise to stay close to me,' Lucy said seriously. 'I saw what those Stinkwaters did to Puss-Pie.'

'Yes, yes — now let's make a plan of campaign. Before this night is over, Biffy is going to know the truth about Everlasting Prendergast!'

Lucy told her mother she was at Cat's house. Cat told her mother she was at Lucy's house. It was a very silly deception — as Lucy pointed out, if anything did happen to them, nobody would know where they were. She also pointed out that if any parent caught them at it, they would be in mega-trouble. But Cat would not be talked out of it. And since Lucy was as determined as she was to convince Biffy, she was easy to persuade.

At five o'clock, everything was in place. Tingling with excitement, they went into Cat's bedroom. Cat picked up the Professor's stone. She and Lucy caught each other's solemn faces, and burst into giggles.

'Good luck, Captain Girlcat,' Lucy said. She

stopped giggling. 'You – you will be careful, won't you?'

'Oh, stop fussing – even if I do get caught, you'll easily beat off a bunch of little cats!' Cat lay down on the stone and began to shrink into a cat. While she was still giddy from the whirlwind of magic, Lucy gently picked her out of the heap of human clothes.

'Don't forget,' she told the small ginger cat, 'mew as loud as you can if you spot any danger.' She sighed. 'It does feel strange, talking to a cat – can you really understand me?'

Cat nodded her little tangerine head. Lucy was delighted. 'This is like a dream. I always wanted to have a conversation with a cat!'

Swiftly and silently, she carried Cat downstairs. Cat heard her parents chatting in the kitchen. Lucy crept to the front door. They had hidden an open tin of tuna (in oil, not brine) on the tiled floor behind Cat's wellies. Lucy picked this up – careful not to slop out the oil – let herself out of the front door and hurried into the street.

'Phew,' she muttered to Cat, 'this oil's getting every-where – I'm going to pong of tuna for a week!'

Cat was not listening. Her senses were stunned and ravished by the scent of paradise. She could almost see the beautiful smell with its proud, silvery tuna face. It made her faint and crazy with longing. She had to have that tuna.

'Cat!' gasped Lucy, whisking the tin out of reach of Cat's paws. 'What are you doing? Get some self-control!'

'Give it to me!' shrieked Cat. It came out as an angry mew. 'Give me that tuna, you – you SKUGG! You KREBBINS!' She tried to run up Lucy's sleeve towards the tantalizing tin.

Lucy held the tin in one hand, and squeezed Cat hard with the other. Her gentle voice was unusually strict. 'Pull yourself together, or this whole mission is cancelled!'

Cat stopped struggling and swiping. The human part of her was ashamed – she had let her lowest cat instincts get the better of her. She had hurled words of cattish abuse that she didn't even know she knew. But she had to be strong enough to rise above the temptation of the delicious tuna. She licked Lucy's arm, in a way she hoped was apologetic.

'That's OK,' said Lucy, who seemed to understand her remarkably well. 'Just don't do it again.'

They were on the corner of Tunnock Avenue. As they had agreed, Lucy put Cat down on the pavement. On her tiny paws, Cat trotted past the open door of the Admiral Tunnock. Lucy followed, clutching the smelly, slippery tin of tuna. The pub was quiet. Cat led Lucy down a narrow alley to a small yard behind the pub kitchen. She hid herself carefully (and somewhat uncomfortably) in a large wooden case of empty bottles.

Lucy had wanted to know what signal she should give, to tell Shouter Prendergast she was there. Cat had said she wouldn't need a signal, because the powerful smell of tuna would bring him out. Sure enough, after less than a minute, the fat form of Everlasting Prendergast waddled through the open door.

Behind her screen of bottles, Cat shuddered. The saintly Shouter looked quite different when he thought no other cat was watching. His black face was cold and calculating. Even his smug, buttery smell was different – hot and sour, like burnt plastic. It was more obvious every minute that Lucy's suspicions had been spot on.

Lucy placed the open tin of tuna on the ground. As arranged, she left the yard to watch from the bottom of the alley. Everlasting Prendergast, however, didn't wait until the human had gone. His face went straight into the tuna, cleverly avoiding the sharp edges of the tin. He licked and snapped at the tuna like an expert, dragging out great chunks with his pointed teeth.

In an amazingly short time, the tin was empty. The reverend let out a resounding burp. Cat watched impatiently while he washed his face – when was the porky old gangster going to get off his bum and lead

 127

her to the enemy? At last, he strolled slowly back into the pub.

Action stations. Cat leapt after him, using all her cattish and human senses to keep him in sight without being seen. The loud, yeasty smells in the pub were very confusing. Cat was glad when they got out into the street. Now she could concentrate on Prendergast. She knew they were coming into enemy territory now. Her heart hammered with fear – evil Stinkwater smells were swooping around her. She longed to run home, but she couldn't give up the unmasking of the Reverend.

Prendergast went through an open front gate and along a path down the side of a large house. The human side of Cat was dismayed, because she recognized the house of Mrs Coombes, headmistress of her school. But this was nothing to the terror of her cattish side, when she caught the fearsome reek of Major Mincible. This was Mincible's land, and she was in very serious danger.

Where was Lucy? Cat flung a look over her shoulder, and could not see her. It was too late to turn back now. She followed Prendergast into a back garden. Stinkwater smells and voices were loud behind a wooden shed. Trying not to think about the risk she was taking – and praying that Lucy at least knew where she was – Cat crouched behind a large watering can.

If she peeped a little way round the rusty spout of

the watering can, she could see the gathering of Stinkwaters. Darson and his chief wife, Sleeza, were here. So was the handsome, sinister Major Mincible. Cat also recognized three cats she had seen around the neighbourhood – a pair of slender, exotic Siameses, and an extremely fluffy white cat who looked like a burst pillow. There was no sign of either Crasho or Vartha.

'Advance, Prendergast,' said Major Mincible. 'What news do you bring us?'

'Whew,' said Prendergast, 'it's close today, don't you find?' He sat down. 'I'm afraid I've brought another demand from the Cockledusters.' (All the Stinkwater cats groaned.) 'This time, the fiends want ten good big moths and two young pigeons – still alive, if possible, but not struggling too much.'

'I'll put my best hunters on it,' Darson said. 'How is my Vartha?'

The reverend was shifty. 'Oh, fine. As long as you keep sending the food, the Cockledusters won't kill her.'

Cat nearly gasped out loud. The LIES! She had never heard such a brazen pack of them. Prendergast was using the disappearance of Crasho and Vartha to blackmail BOTH SIDES! Did he know where they were? And which side was he on, anyway?

'Well, I'll be off, then,' said Everlasting Prendergast. He stood up, shaking his ears.

Major Mincible blocked his path. 'Not so fast!'

'We're getting very tired of waiting!' hissed Darson. 'Where's the Sardine?'

The reverend was shiftier than ever, but very dignified. 'My dear Darson, don't be ignorant. The Blessed Sardine won't come when you call. It must be COAXED. It must be LURED.' He burped. 'Pardon me! I shall get it as soon as I can – I'm saying special summoning-prayers tonight.'

'DOGPLOP!' Mincible said rudely. 'Tell it to hurry up. Because if I see you here again WITHOUT it, I'm going to rip your furry belly open – and I'm going to kick you into the country so fast you won't know you've left!'

'That would be rather silly of you,' Prendergast said, still cool. 'You can't kill me before you've got the Sardine, can you?'

'Don't count on it!' shouted Darson. 'If I find you've been lying to me – well, let's hope you like COUNTRY AIR!'

'I smell something,' Sleeza put in suddenly. Her small pink nose sniffed the air greedily. Her head turned in every direction, until she fastened on to Cat's smell. 'Joy and rapture! I smell kill-kill-kill!'

Cat had turned to stone. Her blood hummed in her ears. Sleeza was hungry for a murder. Her scent grabbed at Cat, seconds before her paw did.

Cat tried to scream. No sound came out. Sleeza's bony paw was across her mouth and she could hardly breathe.

'It's the GIRLCAT!' she screamed. 'And she's MINE! I claim the distinction of killing a human!'

Like a sign from heaven, a human voice boomed above them. 'Let's see if she's run into my garden.'

It was Mrs Coombes, the headmistress, marching briskly up her garden path. Beside her – to Cat's dizzy relief and delight – was Lucy. Had shy Lucy actually dared to ring Mrs Coombes's doorbell? The head-mistress was a stern, stately person, and even the teachers at Bagwell Park Primary were a little scared of her.

The two Siamese cats, Everlasting Prendergast and Sleeza streaked away over the wall. Mrs Coombes loomed over the Stinkwater meeting in time to see the fluffy white cat.

'Bathmat!' she scolded. 'Get back next door at once!'

'Here she is,' Lucy said. 'That's my cat!' She leaned over and scooped Cat into her arms.

Mrs Coombes (smiling and seeming really very nice) said, 'Oh, I'm so glad you found her. And isn't she pretty? I've never seen a ginger with such lovely markings. What's her name?'

'Er – Maud,' said Lucy, only hesitating for a second.

'Charming.' Mrs Coombes stroked Major Mincible. 'This naughty boy is my Jacko.'

'He's beautiful,' Lucy said truthfully.

'Yes, and he's such a softy – just a big kitten!'

Lucy politely thanked Mrs Coombes. She carried Cat out of the garden, holding her very tightly. In the street, they saw Major Mincible through the sitting room window, playing with an old sock. He gave them a look of pure poison, which made Cat shudder.

'You were in trouble, weren't you?' whispered Lucy into Cat's delicate ear. 'I recognized that beautiful striped cat – that was Mincible, wasn't it? Were they trying to kill you?'

Cat nodded her head vigorously.

'I came as quickly as I could. I'd better take you home now, hadn't I?'

The small orange cat nodded again. The human part of Cat thought about toast and Marmite. A second later, however, all human thoughts flew out of her head. A smell had crossed their path. The fat form of Prendergast was sneaking along the street, keeping under hedges and dodging behind dustbins, so that no other cat would spot him. There would never be a better chance to follow him and find out where he was hiding the Blessed Sardine.

Cat jumped out of Lucy's arms and shot away along the pavement.

'Where are you going?' cried Lucy. 'Cat! What are you playing at? Have you gone mad? Come back!'

Cat wished she could explain, but there was no time. In the fading afternoon light, she kept her green eyes fixed on the huge furry backside of Everlasting Prendergast.

10
BEING A PLINKY

When they passed the Windy Terribles, the criminal cat slowed down. Cat could hear him huffing and puffing – he was too fat to run very far. He turned into the part of the land the humans called Victory Street. This was a blank and lonely road. The windowless wall of the Greek bakery was on one side, and the old railway line on the other. Prendergast was heading for the railway line. After one more careful look around, he squeezed through a gap in the sagging wire fence.

Cat hesitated. It might be absolutely mad to follow him into this sinister place. The railway had not been used for years, so she wouldn't have to worry about being run over by a train. But there was a large sign on the fence: 'DANGER! KEEP OUT!', and the weeds towered as high above her as office blocks.

Cat knew, as everyone did, that the old railway was where the wild cats lived. She had often seen these dirty, surly animals, without collars or bells, skulking around the wheely-bins at the flats. Someone had written to the local newspaper, complaining that the wild cats were a 'menace' to respectable pets. Cat was not sure she fancied meeting one. On the other hand, it would be a shame to give up now. Trying to look brave, she trotted towards the hole in the fence.

'No! You can't go in there!' Lucy caught up with her, rather out of breath. 'Please be reasonable. If your parents knew you were hanging round the old railway, they'd be frantic.'

'Sorry,' mewed Cat. She jumped through the gap in the fence and vanished into the great, cabbage-smelling jungle of weeds.

The ground under her paws was ashy and full of little pieces of glass and metal. The weeds sloped down to the railway track. Cat hid herself in the shadow of a pile of rubbish. The track was heaped with rubbish – coils of rusted wire, piles of dented oil-drums, twisted supermarket trolleys and legless bits of furniture. Everlasting Prendergast sauntered along the track, and stopped at the black opening of the old tunnel.

Cat shuddered. She hated tunnels. They were horribly dark, and you never knew what might be lurking inside them.

A rough tomcat voice growled, 'Who goes there? I smell PLINKY!'

'Of course you do,' Prendergast said. 'It's ME. The HOLY Plinky. Let me in, Swugg. We mustn't keep your mother waiting.'

'Huh,' said Swugg, 'that's never bothered you before.' He stepped out of the tunnel. Cat saw that his fur was a peculiar patchwork of ginger and black. 'The old girl's cross with you!'

Swugg whisked round and ran into the tunnel. Prendergast paused to arrange his mean face into a smirk. Then he followed.

Cat took several deep breaths to steady her hammering heart, and crept after them. The inside of the tunnel was not as dark as she had feared. She could make out a large, silent crowd of wild cats, gathered round a broken wooden packing case. On top of this sat the most extraordinary old female that Cat had ever seen. She had only one ear, and the remaining one was ragged. She was wrinkled and crafty, with bald patches in her dingy tabby fur. She looked as if she had died, been badly stuffed and then attacked by moths. Cat pressed herself against the slimy tunnel wall, behind a small pile of bricks. She sensed that this old female was a kind of queen.

Prendergast sat down. 'Ooof! Hello, Spikeletta.'

'And about stigging time,' croaked Spikeletta. 'Where have you been for the past three darks?'

Prendergast's smirk widened. 'I was working, dear – for the two of us, and our powerful future. Don't spoil your fascinating face with a naughty frown!'

Cat thought Spikeletta must be rather a droopag to fall for this rubbish, but she seemed to like it.

'Heh heh heh, you wicked old basket!' she chuckled. 'Are you King of the Plinkies yet?'

'I've got a tiny problem,' said Prendergast. 'May I speak to you alone, my daffodil?'

Spikeletta glanced round at the crowd of wild cats. 'Everybody out!'

The crowd of cats instantly disappeared, as if by magic – Cat trembled to feel several of them whisking past her.

'I said ALONE!' Prendergast started to flick his tail crossly.

A crowd of tough tomcats were still sitting round Spikeletta's packing-case throne.

'My eighteen sons are staying here,' said Spikeletta. 'Isn't that right, boys?'

'Yes, Ma,' muttered the eighteen sons.

Prendergast's oily voice was calm, but his tail flicked harder. 'Now, Spikeletta, don't make a fuss. The Stinkwaters are threatening to kill me – but I can sort it all out if you give me the Blessed Sardine.'

Cat nearly mewed aloud with excitement. Spikeletta had the Sardine! At last she was about to see it!

'Heh heh heh!' cackled Spikeletta. 'No Sardine until

I get my wedding. You promised to marry me and make me Queen!'

'Do be reasonable,' sighed Prendergast. 'I can't declare myself King and get my paws on the Plinky treasure while the Stinkwaters are trying to kill me. Listen...' He stood up, suddenly a very hard and businesslike cat. 'Here's my plan. I'll pretend to take the Sardine to Darson. Your wild cats will then attack and kill him. When we've beaten the Stinkwaters, our army will attack the Cockledusters, killing all the royal family – plus that drivelling old plapp of a General. But first I need the Sardine.'

'First I need the wedding,' said Spikeletta. 'It's not legal unless we do the scratches.'

The reverend stamped his front paw crossly. 'All right! We'll do the scratches tomorrow.'

'Tonight!' hissed Spikeletta. 'Right now!'

Prendergast did not look as if he liked this idea at all. 'If I get the Sardine. You said you'd keep it safe, far from the prying noses of either the Cockledusters or the Stinkwaters. And I'm really very grateful. But now I need it back.'

'Oh yes!' shrieked Spikeletta. She let out a coarse miaouw of laughter. 'You'll get it back, all right!' Her eighteen sons joined in the laughter.

The tunnel rang with this rough, unpleasant sound. Cat saw that Everlasting Prendergast was agitated and nervous. Some of the sons at the back began to punch each other. Then all the cats were fighting and snarling around the wobbling Reverend.

A strange cat voice suddenly murmured in Cat's ear. 'Stay very quiet! You're in danger here – if they find you, they'll kill you. Turn round, and put the end of my tail into your mouth.'

It was an odd voice, like something heard in a dream. Cat turned round, and found herself looking at the back of a thin black cat. She slipped the end of his tail into her mouth, taking care not to bite it.

This strange cat tugged her quickly out of the tunnel and into the forest of huge weeds. He twisted and turned through these for what seemed like miles, until Cat saw a rotting mattress with rusty springs and all the stuffing bursting out. The strange cat stopped in a small clearing. In the middle was a large oil-drum, lying on its side. A large, ragged sheet of plastic hung over the open end. Lumps of concrete anchored it to the ground. There was an old hubcap filled with water. Cat lapped up a few mouthfuls. The strange cat pushed aside his plastic curtain. With his sharp teeth, he dragged a heap of soft white mattress stuffing out of the oil-drum. He pushed this towards Cat. 'Do sit down.'

Cat said nothing. She could only stare. Her rescuer was an elderly but healthy-looking tomcat. Around his neck he wore a dirty, frayed collar. He was pure

 139

black, except for two white circles around his eyes that made him look as if he was wearing glasses. Where had she seen him before? There was something oddly familiar about the shape of his face, but she had never heard of a cat that could fill its own water bowl and make itself a house.

'Who are you?' she whispered.

'They call me "Wizewun",' the old cat said solemnly. 'Don't be afraid. The wild ones won't bother us here. I'm a Plinky, like you, but they've learned to trust me.'

'What's a Plinky?'

'It's their word for a domestic cat, one that lives with humans,' said Wizewun.

'But don't you have humans?'

Wizewun was solemn. 'I did have a human once. He was a nice old chap. But one day I came in through the landing window and found him lying dead in his armchair.'

'Oh, poor you!' cried Cat. 'Wasn't there anyone to look after you? Is that why you had to turn wild?'

'To tell the truth,' said Wizewun, 'I didn't feel I wanted another human. So I called an ambulance and came here.'

'You – called an ambulance?' Cat was astonished, and rather afraid. 'Do you mean you dialed 999? Can you speak the human language?'

Wizewun smiled. 'Of course not. But I knew how

to press the 9 button three times, and I mewed a lot until they traced us.'

'But that's brilliant! You're so clever!'

'You seem quite clever yourself,' said Wizewun, staring at her thoughtfully. 'You know a lot about human ways for one so young.'

Cat decided not to tell him her secret. Something about this cat genius made her very uneasy, and she didn't feel she could trust him. 'Not really,' she said. She sat down on the heap of mattress-stuffing. It was extremely comfortable.

'The wild cats are all right when you get to know them,' Wizewun said. 'They've sort of adopted me. I teach them things about the world, and they tell me their ancient wisdom. We don't interfere with each other – but if they find you, I won't be able to stop them tearing you to pieces. I'll take you out as soon as the wedding begins.'

'Thank you,' Cat said.

'In the meantime, let's have a snack.' Wizewun ran into his oil-drum and came out with two lumps of old sausage in his mouth. He gave one to Cat. 'I found this in a dustbin. It's amazing what humans throw away.'

The two cats settled down to eat the sausage and to listen to the wild cats. They had become very quiet. At first, there was nothing to listen to except silence, and the wind rustling in the weeds around them.

 141

Then the singing began — one voice, joined by a hundred more voices. The wild beauty of the music startled Cat. Her cat ear felt it could listen forever.

Wizewun saw her face, and smiled. 'Lovely, isn't it? These cats may look dirty and ignorant — but they carry the wisdom of the ages that the Plinkies have forgotten.' He licked his front paws, and stood up. 'I think it's safe for you to leave now. Follow me.'

Cat followed Wizewun through groves of weeds and past teetering heaps of rubbish. The lawless smell of the wild cats surrounded them, but the brilliant old cat had made himself a network of secret paths.

'Here you are, small cat,' Wizewun said at last, nodding towards the gap in the fence. 'It was charming to meet you, but please don't come back. Another time, I might not be able to save you.'

'Thanks so much,' Cat said. 'You've been really kind.'

Wizewun opened his mouth to say something, but was stopped by a loud and terrible scream from the tunnel.

It was Everlasting Prendergast, screaming, 'NO-O-O-O-O-O!' in a voice of agony.

Wizewun shook his head sadly. 'I hope Spikeletta knows what she's doing.'

Cat had another attack of being scared —

Prendergast was a villain, but she hated to think of him being hurt. 'What's happening?' she asked anxiously.

'Destiny,' said Wizewun.

11
A Night Raid

Lucy was waiting by the gap in the fence, pacing up and down the pavement and looking anxiously at her watch.

She gasped with relief when the small ginger cat appeared. 'Cat! I heard terrible screeches, and I was sure something had happened to you. Are you hurt?'

Cat shook her head.

'I'm so glad you've come out – I didn't know what to do. You can't call the police because some cats are fighting, can you? We'd better get back to your house.'

Cat was very tired, and her cat brain was foggy with new impressions. She was glad to jump into the safety of Lucy's arms. She glanced round for Wizewun, but that strange and brilliant animal had vanished.

It was getting dark. If any parent discovered they were out there would be hell to pay. Lucy hurried along Sedley Terrace with her head down.

Marcus Snow was outside the pub, holding a bowl. 'Widnes!' he called. 'Food! Come and get it!'

Cat remembered the terrible scream she had heard, and felt sorry for Marcus. For all anyone knew, Widnes was lying dead beside the old railway track, murdered by Spikeletta and her eighteen sons.

Marcus said 'Hi,' to Lucy as she hurried past him.

'Hi,' whispered Lucy.

Cat looked over Lucy's arm, and saw that Widnes's bowl was filled with healthy dry cat food. She let out a mew of disgust – from a cat's point of view it looked as depressing as one of Mum's wholemeal breakfasts. If this had been Prendergast's special diet, no wonder he had been driven to blackmail.

Lucy turned the corner into Tunnock Avenue. 'Let's hope we can get back without being seen,' she muttered into Cat's pointed ginger ear.

Unfortunately, someone did see them. Emily Baines was sitting on the wall outside her house, eating crisps. She was alone, without a single member of her gang, and she looked bored. Lucy bowed her head and began to walk faster. But the class cow jumped off the wall, blocking the pavement.

'Hi,' said Emily.

'Hi,' said Lucy.

'Where've you been? Does your mum let you go about on your own?'

'Yes,' Lucy lied.

Emily stared, loudly crunching a crisp. 'I expect it's because she's divorced,' she said. 'She can't cope, so she's just letting you run wild.'

This gigantic rudeness would have turned Cat purple with rage and hurt, but Lucy's pale face revealed nothing. She stroked the cat in her arms soothingly, and did not reply.

'You've got that awful cat from ballet,' Emily remarked. 'Have you adopted it?'

'I'm looking after her for a friend,' said Lucy.

Emily sighed. She scrunched the empty crisp packet into a ball. 'Want to come in?'

Cat let out a mew of surprise – what was Emily playing at?

'No, I – thanks, but I've got to get back,' Lucy said.

'Oh, well.' Emily flopped back on the wall. 'I would've asked you in before. My mum said I should, because she's sorry for you. But you're always with that stupid Cat Williams.'

Lucy gripped Cat harder, to stop her leaping at Emily. 'She's not stupid. She's really nice.'

'You only think so because she was the first person to talk to you,' Emily said. 'That's what happens when you're new. If you're not careful, you get lumbered with the class loser. But I think you should dump her now.'

Lucy was thoughtful. 'What've you got against Cat, anyway? Why don't you like her?'

Emily shrugged and giggled, and drummed her expensive pink trainers against the wall. 'Why?' she echoed. 'Oh, you know. Because she's goofy, and her bum's huge, and her clothes are tragic — and her parents are weird. You could get better friends.'

'I like Cat,' Lucy said calmly. 'She's clever and funny and brave. And she's my best friend, actually.'

When Cat heard this, a rush of happiness washed her fury away. It was official — she had a best friend. Lucy had chosen her, not Emily Baines.

'Suit yourself,' Emily said.

A man's voice suddenly barked angrily inside the house. 'Emily! Where the hell is she? Darling, if she can't even stay in the house while I'm here, you can't be teaching her decent manners! I mean, this is the limit, darling!' He said 'darling' as if it was the name of a person he didn't like. 'She might as well be one of the ghastly kids from the flats!'

It was Emily's dad. Mr Baines was often red-faced and shouting, and Cat remembered that he always seemed to be rushing away somewhere with a briefcase.

Emily's eyes went blank, like windows with drawn curtains. She jumped off the wall. 'See ya.'

Lucy almost ran the rest of the way back to Cat's house, praying the two of them had not been missed. Very fortunately, everything went according to plan.

 147

Lucy hid Cat inside her sweatshirt and rang the door-bell. When Dad answered the door, she mumbled out a pack of lies about changing the sleepover to Cat's house, and Cat being upstairs already.

'Oh, that's fine,' Dad said cheerfully. 'Tell Cat you two can have the telly if you like – we've got the Fosters over to supper.' There were voices and snatches of adult laughter in the kitchen. Dad was chewing, and holding a glass of red wine. He grinned at Lucy as she rushed up to Cat's bedroom. 'Come down if you get bored.'

'Thanks,' said Lucy, thinking boredom would be the least of their problems.

Biffy was chicken-sitting outside the bedroom door. His striped face was anxious. Cat poked her head out of Lucy's sweatshirt, and he leapt to his paws with a snarl of relief.

'Thank the Slimy One! Where on earth have you been? Captain Verripritty, you're a very troublesome and disobedient young officer!'

'Don't get the hump, Biffy,' Cat pleaded urgently. 'I've been to the camp of the wild cats—'

'You've WHAT?' roared Biffy.

'I know who's got the Sardine!'

Before Biffy could reply, Mum called from down-stairs. 'Cat! Come and say hi to the Fosters!'

'Whoops,' muttered Lucy. She called back, 'Just coming!' Then she whispered, 'Hurry!'

Having an official best friend made Cat feel brisk and confident. 'I can't talk now,' she told Biffy. 'I have to meet you later – it's an emergency!'

Biffy frowned. 'Our war committee is having a meeting tonight,' he said, 'in the land of Larfing Silex. I suppose I could take you along – but you'd better not be wasting our time, young Madam.'

'Please, Biffy – you have to listen to me.'

'Cat!' called Mum. She began to walk upstairs.

Cat mewed with alarm and jumped out of Lucy's arms – a tremendous, flying jump right across the room to the bed. She threw herself across the Professor's stone, begging it to let her out of the Temple in double-quick time. The moment her human tongue had grown big enough to form the words, she gasped, 'Coming!'

'She's gone down again,' reported Lucy. 'Phew, that was close!'

Still breathless from the magic, Cat scrabbled into the nearest clothes. 'I wish you'd given me a chance to scratch Emily!' she grumbled. 'That cow – who's she calling goofy? And what did she mean about my clothes? Just because Mum thinks glittery pink stuff is naff!'

'I think Emily's nasty to you because she's jealous of you,' Lucy said quietly.

Cat laughed scornfully. 'Me? Don't be silly! Why would she be jealous of me?'

'Because of your parents,' Lucy said. 'Your mum and dad are so nice. And you heard Emily's dad – he never stops shouting at his wife. My mum says one day they'll find that poor woman under the floorboards. Imagine living with a dad like that.'

Cat was doubtful. It was very strange to feel sorry for horrible Emily Baines. 'She must be used to it.'

'Doesn't mean she likes it,' Lucy said. 'My dad used to shout quite a lot. And I really hated it.'

'Oh.' Cat wanted to say she was sorry, and didn't know how. For the first time, she saw herself as someone like Emily might see her – not a loser, but a fabulously lucky person with two excellent parents who only shouted when they were playing Monopoly. I don't appreciate them enough, she thought. Lucy had made her look at the world from a different angle.

Lucy smiled to show that she was not trying to make Cat feel bad. 'That supper they're having downstairs smells wonderful,' she said. 'D'you think there'll be some left for us?'

'I hope so,' Cat said, giggling. 'I'm starving – all I've had for supper is a cat-portion of mouldy sausage!' She had a real best friend. Lucy had told Emily she was 'brave'. Suddenly, she felt ready to face anything.

Biffy was in a huff when he woke Cat for the meeting with the Prime Minister. He refused to speak to her – he still couldn't believe the saintly Prendergast was a criminal, and he was very cross with Cat for putting her human life in danger.

Together, the two cats trotted through dark and sleeping streets to the land of Larfing Silex. The marmalade Prime Minister's human address was a flat near the shops in Pole Crescent. He lived with a large collie dog, who helpfully held open the cat flap with his mouth and nosed a bowl of snacks round the kitchen floor. The disc on his collar said 'Skipper'. He was introduced as 'Phartong', and spoke the cat language with a thick doggish accent. Cat was a little scared of Phartong's large size, and the noisy way his huge tongue flapped when he drank, until she saw how friendly he was with Larfing Silex. The two animals spoke each other's languages – Larfing Silex even cracked a joke in doggish, which made Phartong chuckle. Cat remembered that dogs and cats had been allies since the War with the Birds.

Elixa Atlas and Tuggard Steggings – the two best cat fighters – were waiting in the Prime Minister's kitchen. Cat told her incredible story (Larfing Silex translated the more complicated words for Phartong). All the cats were astonished – Biffy's mouth hung open for a full five minutes.

'Well I never!' exclaimed Larfing Silex.

'I never trusted that Prendergast,' said Elixa Atlas. 'Phew – I'd like to be a beetle on the ceiling when Princess Bing finds out. She'll go crazy!'

'Girlcat, I was wrong,' Biffy said solemnly. 'I see now that when I refused to listen to you, I was the one putting your life in danger.'

'That's all right.' Cat licked his paw, to show there were no hard feelings. 'But what should we do now?'

'We won't bother to rescue that KREBBINS Prendergast,' growled Biffy. 'He's probably dead already. We've got to get our paws on the Sardine. If this Queen of the wild ones has it, we must raid the camp this very night. Fall in, Atlas and Steggings!'

Larfing Silex, who was rather a clumsy fighter, was glad to be left out of this dangerous mission. Cat and Phartong, however, begged to be included. The dog could not get out of the flat without a human, so everyone ignored him.

Cat refused to be ignored. She told Biffy firmly that he needed her. 'I know it's a risk – but Biffy, I can show you Wizewun's secret paths. You'll be much safer if you take me as your guide.'

In the end, very reluctantly, Biffy agreed. One by one, the patrol – Biffy, Cat, Tuggard Steggings and Elixa Atlas – slipped through Larfing Silex's flap. Out in the street, Biffy surprised Cat by leading them all into a back garden, and snapping, 'Bright bits out!'

Cat didn't understand this order, until she saw the other cats leaping on to a barbecue and rolling around in the heap of grey ashes. Cat copied them, turning herself from a dainty orange cat to a streaky, very dirty grey one. The four ashy cats, invisible in the shadows, sped along silent, empty pavements to the old railway line.

'Stay near me at all times!' ordered Biffy. 'Don't make a move without my permission!' For the first time, his gruff voice softened. 'Take care, little opener – my heart will break if anything happens to you.'

Cat licked his cheek gratefully, happy to stay in the shelter of his smell. Her small, ashy body trembled with fear – but she was excited, too, and wouldn't have missed this for the world. How odd, she thought – as a human girl I've always been a bit of a tumfrit, but being a cat has given me a taste for adventure.

In silence, she led the patrol through the hole in the fence and into the forest of towering weeds. She had been hoping to see Wizewun, but there was no sign of him and she couldn't find his secret house. As they moved nearer to the old tunnel, they heard what sounded like a party. The wild cats were howling an eating-song, full of insulting references to Plinkies.

'Ugh, it makes my fur creep!' whispered Elixa Atlas.

'Disgraceful rabble!' muttered Biffy. 'A bit of tough human service would do them the world of good.'

Very luckily for the Plinkies, the wild cats were too caught up in their party to notice the alien smells. Cat led her friends to an opening in the weeds where they could spy on the strange scene.

Dozens of wild cats – far too many to count – were

running in circles round a tangle of rusty barbed wire. Cat assumed they were chasing something. Then she realized this was a cattish form of dancing. Spikeletta sat on her packing-case. She was eating something in front of her with great relish. Every now and then, with her mouth stuffed full, she joined in the howling.

'We must get the Sardine out of these filthy paws!' Biffy whispered.

The human side of Cat suddenly recognized that Spikeletta was eating a very dead and bloody rat. She could not imagine anything more revolting, and the cat side of her shuddered over Spikeletta's dreadful table manners.

Elixa Atlas let out a gasp of surprise. 'Look – it's Prendergast! They've trapped him inside all that sharp stuff!'

Now it was obvious why the wild cats were dancing round the bundle of barbed wire. Imprisoned inside it was the fat and furious form of Everlasting Prendergast. Whatever the reason for his terrible scream, he was alive.

'Hmm, they haven't killed him yet,' sniffed Biffy.

'Great!' said Steggings. 'We haven't missed the good bit.'

The song ended. The dancers stopped.

'Lovely!' cried Spikeletta. The rat's tail drooped from her mouth like a particularly repulsive piece of spaghetti. 'Let's have another!'

Prendergast stood up in his rusty prison, full of outraged dignity. 'That's quite enough. Let me out at once.'

'You listen carefully, you sly old Plinky,' said Spikeletta, 'I'm wise to your tricks now. You made promises to me. I was going to be your Queen, and have a ton of treasure. You said my wild cats would be able to walk in the Plinkies' flaps and eat their posh tinned food. But I'm not keeping a husband who goes around killing my nephews!'

'I've explained about that, Spikeletta – I had to do it, and it was only five of them!'

'You killed five of my best soldiers,' Spikeletta hissed. 'And two of my sisters have stopped speaking to me until I kill you. I'm going to claw your brains out, and then I'm going to make your fur into a nice warm rug.'

Her eighteen sons broke into rough laughter and cheers.

'You can't let her do it!' Cat whispered urgently. Prendergast was her enemy, but when all was said and done he was still a round, furry cat. And she hated to think of his poor human owners.

'I'm going to be King!' shouted Prendergast. 'And you're not going to stop me!'

Spikeletta's battered old head suddenly went still. She sniffed. 'I smell Plinkies at Muck Hill! Seize them!'

Everything happened very fast after this. Cat hardly had time to wonder which bit of the camp was Muck Hill, before a hard black tail smacked across her face. Cat moaned with pain. Strong paws were pushing her along the cindery ground. She tried to struggle, but could not move.

The pain and the pushing stopped as suddenly as it had begun. Cat blinked hard and looked around. She was now right in front of Spikeletta's throne. The other three cats were beside her, heavily guarded by Spikeletta's sons.

'Hello, Biffy,' said Everlasting Prendergast, from his spiked prison. 'How nice of you to drop in.'

Biffy's four legs were trapped, but his whiskers quivered angrily. 'Traitor! YOU were the cat who led my Pokesley to ruin. YOU stole the Blessed Sardine. YOU told the Stinkwaters about the girl-cat.'

'YES!' laughed the criminal cat. 'That Pokesley's a prize-winning young plapp, isn't he? I told him Darson would make him an officer. Hahahaha! They're all fools. I'm cleverer than all of them.'

'That's nice,' said Spikeletta. 'I'll have a CLEVER rug!'

Her eighteen sons laughed and cheered again.

Biffy suddenly let out a great, mewing gasp of amazement. 'By the Fish! I don't believe it!'

Cat asked, 'What's the matter?'

The old cat ignored her. 'Butterbelly! Is it really you?'

Spikeletta stared, then broke into a surprisingly nice smile. 'Nigmo! My very first husband!'

At once, the wild cats let go of their prisoners.

'But Biffy, you're a Plinky!' cried Cat, so astonished that she forgot to be scared. 'Can Plinkies marry wild cats?'

'Oh, it happens all the time,' Spikeletta said. 'All my best soldiers are half-Plinkies. I've had several Plinky husbands – but none of them was a patch on Nigmo!'

'Oh, go along,' mumbled Biffy. Cat saw that he was smiling. 'What an enchanting little rascal you were!'

'My first four sons are yours,' Spikeletta told him happily. 'Boys, come out and meet your pa.'

Four of her hulking, grimy sons slouched out to bow to Biffy. The old General was grinning with all his might.

'Fine lads!' he cried proudly. 'Look at those fat tails!'

'This changes everything,' declared Spikeletta. 'These Plinkies can leave – unless they want to stay for the killing.'

'Butterbelly,' said Biffy, 'don't kill Prendergast – give him to us!'

Spikeletta stared. 'Why d'you want him?'

'Those of us who live with the humans have different

 157

customs,' explained Biffy. 'This wicked cat must have a TRIAL. It is the law in our land.'

'Oh, Biffy,' sighed Spikeletta. 'I never could say "No" to you! Boys — wrap the prisoner up nicely.'

'Yes, Ma!'

Cat watched, fascinated. Spikeletta's eighteen sons surrounded the barbed-wire prison. All you could see was a wall of furry backs, in every kind of colour and stripe. But there were terrible yowls, and signs of a hard paw-to-paw struggle. The sons stood back, to reveal Everlasting Prendergast lashed into a ball with metres of green gardening twine. His four legs and his tail were tied tightly to his fat body, making him look like a huge, wobbly, furry egg. There was an old apple core jammed into his mouth. His eyes were slits of rage.

'Thank you,' Biffy said, flourishing his tail at Spikeletta.

'I've still got that lovely dead mouse you gave me,' Spikeletta said coyly. 'It went hard.'

'I must call again and catch up on all your news.'

'Any time, Nigmo,' said Spikeletta. She flicked her tail at the struggling, trussed-up Prendergast. 'Boys — roll him to the border!'

Her eighteen sons moved like a furry machine. Forming themselves into ranks, they rolled the egg-shaped prisoner along a network of overgrown paths. They rolled him right to the fence, and squeezed him through the hole. Then, without saying goodbye, the wild cats disappeared into the night.

On the pavement of Victory Street, Biffy gazed down at Prendergast. 'What the scales are we going to do with this splodge of evil? We'll never roll him home!'

At last, Prendergast managed to spit out the apple core. 'You don't have to – untie me, and I can walk. I promise not to run away.'

'Rubbish!' shouted Elixa Atlas, her fur bristling angrily.

'I can tell you where to find the Blessed Sardine. I sold it this afternoon, to Darson Stinkwater.'

'NO!' yelled Tuggard Steggings. 'It's a pack of lies! It's at the wild camp! The girlcat heard you say so.'

Prendergast smirked. 'I only hid the Sardine with Spikeletta for a short time, because I didn't think any of my usual places would be safe.'

'But Spikeletta put you in prison,' said Cat. 'Why? And why did you give that terrible scream at your wedding?'

'Oh, that.' Prendergast looked annoyed, and a little embarrassed. 'Well, if you must know, I screamed because I'd just heard something awful. You see, there were one or two delays to our wedding, and Spikeletta unfortunately got into one of her tempers. So she gave the Sardine to one of her nephews. And he ATE

 159

IT. That's why I screamed — after all that effort, the Blessed Sardine was inside one of those great louts.'

'What?' gasped Biffy. He, Tuggard and Elixa Atlas were statues of horror. 'He ATE the Blessed Sardine?'

'So how did you get it back to sell it to the Stinkwaters?' demanded Cat.

'I did the only thing I could,' Prendergast said coolly. 'It was dangerous, but there wasn't any other way. One by one, I lured Spikeletta's nephews right to the bottom of the tunnel, murdered them and slit open their bellies.'

All the cats gasped, astonished by such wickedness.

Prendergast grinned, pleased with the effect he was having. 'You know, some cats assume I'm too fat to be a good fighter. But that is a very serious mistake. I found the Sardine when I got to Number Five — to my relief, since Spikeletta had fifty-nine nephews at the last count and even I get tired. Then I sold it to Darson.' He scowled. 'Everything would have been fine, if only I'd had time to hide the dead bodies. How was I to know I'd killed them in the place where the old droopag hides her rat-bones? She told her sons and they hunted me down.'

The casual way he talked about the murders made Cat feel sick. 'What can we do with him?' she asked Biffy. 'I know his humans will be worried — but we can't set him free! We can't let him kill again!'

'That's the human in you,' Prendergast said. 'Killing comes more naturally to us cats.'

'Speak for yourself,' Biffy said sternly.

'You'd better untie me,' said the murderous Prendergast. 'I know where the Stinkwaters have hidden the Sardine. And I know their battle plans. If I don't tell you, you're finished. Let's face it, Biffy – I'm your only hope.'

'Don't listen to him!' shouted Cat. 'He's lying!'

The other three cats were silent for a long moment, looking doubtfully down at the trussed-up Shouter.

'He's right,' Biffy sighed. 'Whether he's lying or not, beating the Stinkwater invasion and winning back the Sardine is our only chance to save the Cockledusters. You'd better untie him.'

Elixa Atlas and Tuggard Steggings set to work with their teeth, biting through the gardening twine around the fat cushion that was Prendergast. Cat and Biffy kept watch. Along the street, there was human activity beside the Greek Bakery. Two men were loading plastic crates into a large lorry. They took no notice of the cats.

'Done it!' cried Steggings, as he snapped the last piece of string.

'Grab him!' shrieked Cat.

But it was too late. The moment he was free, Prendergast leapt to his feet and made a dash for the lorry.

 161

'You won't catch me for your stinky trial!' he yelled over his shoulder. 'YOU'LL be the ones on trial – in a STINKWATER court! Darson's got the Sardine safe in his human's house, where it's guarded day and dark! And they're planning the invasion for Saturday dark! Hahahaha! But I'm not telling you WHERE!'

The villainous cat could move very fast when he wanted to. He leapt into the lorry, just a few seconds before one of the men shut the door. The great motor rumbled into life, and the lorry roared away round the corner.

'Oh, SQUETT!' swore Tuggard Steggings.

Elixa Atlas nudged him. 'Language!'

With her human senses, Cat read the writing on the side of the lorry: 'LONDON – FELIXSTOWE – ROTTERDAM'.

They would not be seeing Prendergast again. The wicked cat who had thrown the whole cat nation into turmoil was going on a very long journey.

12
At Last

The Cockleduster cats had got rid of the dreadful Prendergast, but there was no time for rejoicing. The Blessed Sardine was in the paws of the enemy, and the Stinkwaters were planning an invasion. Cat shivered with anxiety. What would happen to her beloved Cockleduster cats if the Stinkwaters won this ridiculous war?

Biffy stood on the kerb staring at where the lorry had been. Then he shook his head until his baggy old ears slapped together, as if trying to clear it, and turned back to his soldiers.

'Pay attention, cats. Prendergast is a liar, but we have to assume he's telling the truth about the Sardine. If there is an invasion next Saturday dark, we must be prepared.'

'He said Darson's hidden the Sardine in his human's house' shouted Elixa Atlas. 'Let's go round there and dive through his flap!'

'We wouldn't get near it,' Biffy said. 'It's always surrounded by Darson's flap-guards. No — we'll have to break into the house and rescue the Sardine BEFORE Saturday.'

Cat said nothing, but felt even more worried. Did Biffy realize this was next to impossible? How could a group of cats break into a human house without using the cat flap?

'We'd better have another meeting tomorrow dark,' Biffy said, 'to make a plan of campaign. Back to your lands, everyone — and spread the word about Prendergast!'

Cat was very tired by now. Ashy and yawning, she trailed through the deserted streets behind Biffy, trying to think of ways to rescue the Blessed Sardine. She and Lucy discussed it all the next day, whenever they could talk without any parent hearing.

'I hate to sound mean,' Cat said, 'but we have to face it — the cats are far too silly to manage this on their own. We'll have to make a plan for them. And I haven't a clue how to do it.'

It was the afternoon, and Mrs Church had taken Lucy and Cat to the swimming pool. They were sitting in the toddlers' pool, taking the chance to talk while Lucy's mum was doing lengths.

'This is where my great mind comes in useful,' Lucy said. 'We can end this war if cats and humans work together. There's got to be a way.' She frowned, her great mind working busily. 'Darson has planned the invasion for next Saturday, right?'

'That's right,' Cat said gloomily. 'He'll bring the Sardine and declare himself King. We can't stop him unless we get the Sardine first. And we can't get the Sardine unless we BURGLE Emily's house. It's hopeless.'

'You're forgetting,' Lucy said, 'that on Friday – the day before Darson's invasion – Emily's having a birthday party.'

'So?'

'Don't you see?' asked Lucy. 'That'll be the perfect time to snatch the Sardine, when Emily's house is full of people!'

'But you refused to be in her gang and she thinks I'm goofy,' Cat pointed out. 'There's no way she'll invite either of us near her party!'

Lucy smiled mysteriously. 'There are always ways and means,' she said.

Over the next few days, Cat's parents and Lucy's mother were puzzled by the strange behaviour of the two best friends. Suddenly, Cat and Lucy had stopped walking to school together. Whenever other people were watching, Lucy coldly ignored Cat. At school, she refused to speak to her. She hung about on the fringes of Emily's gang, and joined in the titters when Emily made jokes about Cat's bum. After school, the two girls walked home without a word and went into their separate houses.

The moment they were sure that nobody in Emily's gang could see them, however, they stopped pretending. Lucy climbed over the trellis into Cat's garden, and they talked as hard as ever.

'I'll never understand ten-year-old girls,' Dad said. 'Are you ALL bonkers?'

Lucy felt bad about even pretending not to like Cat. 'Please try to forget it – I don't mean a word of it.'

'I know,' Cat said. Lucy's pretending was surprisingly painful – it reminded Cat how lonely she had been without a best friend. But she was determined to be brave about it. If Emily found out they were still talking, the whole plan was doomed.

On Thursday afternoon, Lucy went to Woolworth's and bought a new CD by a boy-band Emily liked. She wrapped it in pink paper (Emily's favourite colour) and went down the street to Emily's house.

Cat waited anxiously in her garden. She jumped up as soon as Lucy's face appeared through the trellis. 'Well?'

'Success,' Lucy said. She was beaming. 'Emily's mum opened the door. When she saw that I'd come round with a birthday present, she more or less forced

Emily to invite me to her party. I think it's because my parents are divorced. So you see, there are some advantages.'

Her coolness took Cat's breath away. 'You're so funny,' she said admiringly. 'Not in a ha-ha way – I mean, you seem so quiet and serious, but you've somehow got a party-invitation out of your worst enemy, in less than a week!'

Lucy laughed and turned faintly pink at Cat's stumbling compliments. 'I'm so happy that I can do something useful for the cats. I would love to end this war – why can't the Cockledusters and Stinkwaters just be FRIENDS?'

'For the same reason we can't be friends with Emily,' Cat said firmly. 'Darson Stinkwater is a terrible cat, and if we don't come up with a good plan, he'll kill my Biffy.' Her voice faltered. She could never bear to think of Biffy's journey to the country.

Lucy squeezed her hand kindly. 'I'm way ahead of you. Listen carefully – this is what you must tell the cats to do . . .'

The cats had never had leadership like this. Lucy had thought of everything. ('What a brain!' cried Biffy. 'Wasted on a human!') All through Thursday night and Friday, Biffy worked his way around the neighbouring streets, visiting every Cockleduster sympathizer and raising an army. Cat and Lucy told

 167

their parents they were with each other – a foolish thing to do, as they had agreed last time they did it, but this was an emergency.

At six o'clock on Friday, when the afternoon sunlight was fading, Lucy left for Emily's party. Anyone who had been watching the street closely would have seen that the shadows were full of dark shapes. A stream of cats, from as far off as the flats in Hopton Street, made their way towards the Watsons' back garden. They slipped over fences, leapt across dustbins, trotted through flower-beds and along gutters.

Lucy saw them when she walked along Tunnock Avenue to Emily's party. It was a strange sight – dozens and dozens of swift, silent cats, coming from every direction and pouring into the same place.

Someone mewed at her feet. Lucy looked down. A small ginger cat glowed in the warm light of the early summer evening.

'Good luck, Cat,' Lucy said. 'Be careful!'

Cat briefly rubbed herself against Lucy's ankles, and ran to join the crowd of cats in the Watsons' garden. This meeting-place had been chosen partly because it was the land of the dying King, and partly because Mr and Mrs Watson were too old to go outside – at this time of year, there was always a risk that humans would decide to have a barbecue.

Cat's first task was to crouch on the sill and watch

the clock through the kitchen window – the success of the whole operation depended upon her being the only cat in the world who could tell the time.

'Why is she staring at that round thing on the wall?' wondered Elixa Atlas.

'Now!' mewed Cat, leaping off the sill. 'We've got five minutes to get to Emily's!'

'Five minutes' meant nothing to the cats, but they all understood Biffy's long snarl of 'Atten – SHUN!'

If any human had been watching, they would have been amazed to see how fast the cats organized themselves into an army.

'Here are your orders – get into the human house as soon as the girlcat's friend opens the door!' Biffy cried. 'Good luck, everyone. Muffle bells!'

'WAIT!' cried an old cat voice.

The Watsons' cat flap clattered as something pushed against it. There was a sound of tremendous huffing and puffing.

'Great Scales!' gasped Prince Cockie, 'it's FATHER!'

It was indeed the stout, tabby form of the dying King. Biffy rushed to the flap to help pull him through. The cats stared in silence as the King squeezed himself out into the garden, coughing slightly in the unfamiliar air. His legs trembled and his whiskers drooped, but his old face was full of a warlike pride.

'A King's place is at the head of his army!' he declared. 'I have come out to LEAD the invasion!'

'But Your Majesty, you're far too ill!' argued Biffy. 'You can't leave your basket!'

'Biffy, my old friend,' wheezed the King, 'sometimes a royal cat must simply do his duty. Remember, cats – GLORY or DEATH , but NO SURRENDER!'

There was a moment of stillness, then the voice of Tuggard Steggings yelled, 'Nine cheers for the King!'

And King Cockleduster the Ninth smiled fatly as the Watsons' garden rang with cat cheers. Cat was proud to be marching behind the fine old warrior. He couldn't do much, but his brave appearance seemed to give all the cats extra strength and courage.

'PLACES!' roared Biffy.

The cats lined up behind their King and poured in a steady stream of multi-coloured fur towards the land of Darson Stinkwater.

At Emily's house, a large bunch of pink balloons was tied to the front door-knocker. From inside, Cat heard thumping music and over-excited voices. Her pulse galloping, she joined the pack of cats waiting on the path.

Lucy had calculated the time perfectly. Just as the cats took their places, she opened the Baines's front door.

The old King lifted one paw and shot out his claws. 'CHARGE!' he shouted.

In a great tidal wave of fur, the Cockleduster army surged past Lucy into the Baines's house. Elixa Atlas led a search party upstairs. Tuggard Steggings led a group of tough toms to the kitchen. The rest swarmed into the sitting room, where a big table was laid with party food – including a gigantic pink birthday cake, with eleven glittery pink candles and the words 'Happy Birthday Emily' spelled out in tiny white marshmallows.

The party guests (the five permanent members of Emily's gang) shrieked. Emily's mum shrieked. The invading cats nearly knocked her over, and she scattered crisps all over the carpet. The King immediately began to eat the crisps.

Emily's dad yelled, 'What's going on? Where the hell have all these cats come from?' He dived to grab the nearest cat. 'AARGH!' He had made the mistake of grabbing Princess Bing, who gave him a hard bite on the thumb and wriggled neatly out of his grasp. Mr Baines blundered about, shouting and sucking his wound.

Mrs Baines cried, 'DO something! Call the police!'

The cats were searching every centimetre of the room. When Emily's mother tried to push them away from her soft furnishings, they snapped and hissed.

'They're trying to KILL us!' screamed Emily.

Cat knew she did not have much time. As they had agreed, Lucy picked her up and carried her around the house so that she could sniff for the Blessed Sardine in relative safety. She sniffed Darson's basket in the utility room, his water bowl on the kitchen floor and the wine-rack under the stairs where he kept a cushion. There was no sign of the Sardine.

On the landing, halfway up the stairs, Lucy said, 'Oh, no!'

Through the landing window, Cat saw another column of cats running through the Baines's back garden. She let out a sharp mew. Darson's flap-guards had raised the alarm, and handsome Major Mincible was leading a large, ferocious Stinkwater army. One by one, as fast as beads falling off a necklace, the Stinkwater cats jumped through the flap and into the fight.

The Baines house was in CHAOS.

On every chair, on every stair, on every bed, chair, table and floor, cats were spitting and snarling and wrestling. Claws ripped into sofa cushions, and the sitting room was in a snowstorm of white feathers.

'Call the RSPCA!' cried Mrs Baines. 'Call the Zoo!'

Emily and two of her gang members clung together, trembling, as the cats clawed and spat around them. The other three members of Emily's gang ran away through the open front door.

'I'm calling the Council Pest Controller!' shouted Mr Baines. The fighting cats had crowded him into a corner, and he was trying to shove them aside with a broom. 'These are PESTS all right! Worse than RATS!'

Tuggard Steggings and Major Mincible jumped on the food table. They locked their teeth into each other's necks. With a loud SQUELCH, Steggings rolled on top of a green jelly covered with whipped cream. Lumps of sweet gloop plopped out of his fur on to the carpet. One dropped beside the King, who began to lick it. Mincible overturned a bowl of small chocolate cakes. The King burped, and curiously tasted a cake.

A spitting Sleeza chased Elixa Atlas downstairs. 'Keep searching, Girlcat!' Elixa gasped.

She jumped on to the piano. Sleeza jumped after her. They struggled on the keys, adding tuneless, jangling music to the general din.

'Ow!' Lucy gasped suddenly, as Stinkwater claws dug into her ankle. She dropped Cat into the mass of fighting fur.

Cat let out a jagged mew of alarm. She was terrified, but she struck out bravely at the cats who pounced on her. She managed to back away towards the hall.

Mr Baines – still trying to swipe cats with his broom – was shouting down the phone, 'Yes, I said cats! No, you did hear me properly – HUNDREDS of cats!'

'Take your filthy paws off my human!' roared a

 173

beloved voice. If Cat had been a girl, she would have wept with relief. Biffy had come to rescue her. There was a large blob of jelly on the top of his head, like a wobbly green hat, but it only added to his authority. He biffed his way through the furred tangle of Stinkwaters. Two of them ran away up the curtains.

'Get them off my new curtains!' screeched Mrs Baines.

'Girlcat! Did they hurt you?'

'Oh, I'm fine – I haven't found the Sardine—'

Suddenly, out of the snarling and screaming confusion, a humble cat voice spoke to them.

'Father!'

Biffy's tabby-and-white body stiffened angrily.

Cat recognized the voice. 'It's Pokesley!'

'Please, Father – don't you know me?' The dentist's cat was crouching under the sofa. Only the tip of his nose and the ends of his paws were visible.

Biffy scowled. 'I don't know any Stinkwaters!'

'I'm not a Stinkwater any more,' Pokesley said. 'I hate them, and I'm sorry I ever listened to Darson. I don't care what they do to me – I'm giving you the Sardine!'

'You're coming back!' cried Cat. 'Oh, Pokesley, that's wonderful! Please forgive him now, Biffy!'

'I don't know if I can trust him,' Biffy said. His voice was stern, but Cat could see that he was wavering. He

174

had missed his foolish son, and in his heart, was sorry he had ever called him a plapp.

'Please take me back, Father!' begged Pokesley. 'I just want Darson to lose and the war to be over and everything to be nice again!'

'Do you really know where he's hidden the Sardine?'

'Follow me.' Pokesley slid out from under the sofa and dashed into the hall. Cat and Biffy dashed after him. He led them up the stairs – past Lucy, who was sitting on the bottom stair wiping the blood off her scratched ankle. She jumped up when she saw Cat and Biffy, and went after them.

'It's at the very top,' Pokesley panted over his shoulder. 'He hid it there when the wild cats sold it to him.'

'But he must have guards around it,' Biffy said suspiciously. 'If this is a TRAP—'

'No, Father – truly! The guards are fighting in the washing-place!'

Sure enough, as the three cats and Lucy reached the top landing, they heard terrible snarls and crashes from the bathroom. Pokesley led them quickly into a very pink bedroom. Despite the emergency, Cat couldn't help looking round curiously. Emily's bedroom was stuffed with luxuries. There were racks of videos, pictures of ponies, a telephone (pink) and even a pink sink. Pokesley jumped on to the frilly dressing table, which was crowded with boxes and bottles. He patted a white box with his paw.

'In here! Help me get it open!' He fumbled at it clumsily.

Lucy saw what he was trying to do, and leaned forward to open the white box. A little plastic ballerina popped up and the box played a tinkly tune. It was filled with beads and rings and tiny bottles of pink and mauve nail varnish – and something else.

Biffy made a huffing sound which was the cat version of a gasp.

There, among the glitter, lay a small hard brown thing – like a fish wrapped in old, stiff bandages. Cat remembered when Dad had taken her to the Egyptian gallery at a museum in Oxford. There had been a mummified cat in a glass case, with a mummified fish beside it. This object was exactly the same. It could only be the Blessed Sardine.

There was no time to wonder how the Cockleduster cats had got hold of an Egyptian mummy.

'Pokesley, my boy,' cried Biffy, 'I'm sorry I ever doubted you. If we get out of here alive, I'm making you an officer!'

'Good heavens!' said the voice of Lucy, above them. 'It really is a sardine!' Very carefully she picked it up.

'Don't be afraid,' Cat told the others, 'it'll be safer if a human has it.'

'Oh, I trust Queenie's human,' Biffy assured her.

Lucy and the cats hurried downstairs. The guards in the bathroom ran after them, but fell back with yowls of horror when they saw the captured Sardine in Lucy's hand. In a second, they had bellowed out the news – 'They've got it! The Cockledusters have got the Sardine!'

'NOT FOR LONG!' screeched a dreadful voice. Something black shot through the air like a furry missile. Lucy screamed. Darson had ripped the Sardine right out of her hand.

Cat, Biffy and all the Cockledusters let out howls of anguish – lost again!

'Hahahaha!' shrieked Sleeza.

'Yeuch,' said Mr Baines. 'What the hell has that cat got in his mouth?' He leaned forward and tugged the Blessed Sardine out of Darson's mouth. It crumbled between Darson's teeth and came out in a shower of brown ashes. 'Ugh, how DISGUSTING!' said Mr Baines. 'Whatever it is, it's heaving with germs!'

He jerked open the door of the downstairs bathroom and flushed the Blessed Sardine down the toilet.

The effect was astonishing. Suddenly, every cat in the house was as still and silent as a statue.

'What? What?' muttered Mr Baines.

'What's happened?' whispered Mrs Baines. 'Why have they suddenly gone quiet?'

'This changes everything,' Darson said. 'The Sardine has vanished. So who has won?'

 177

Green jelly slid down Biffy's tragic face. 'Vanished!' he croaked.

'You Stinkwaters can't invade us now!' shouted Tuggard Stuggings.

'No — and you Cockledusters can't invade us, either,' said Major Mincible. 'This is all very puzzling.'

'The battle may be over,' Darson said, 'but not the war. Without the Sardine, our borders aren't worth the soil they're scratched in. I demand a meeting with your KING.'

'That won't be possible,' said Elixa Atlas. Cat saw that she was crying. 'Not where he is now!'

It was too true. The dead body of King Cockleduster the Ninth lay in the ruins of Emily's birthday cake, his crumby face stretched into an enormous smile.

13
STAR-CROSS'D LOVERS

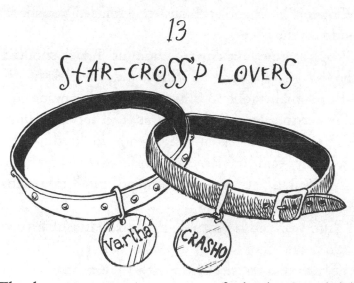

The humans were in a state of shock. Cat didn't blame them. The Baines's house was wrecked. The air was full of whirling feathers from burst cushions. There were long scratches all over the furniture, and blots of food mashed into the carpets. Emily, her mother and the remaining party guests clung together, shivering. Though Cat was full of grief for the King, she had some sympathy to spare for Emily – nobody deserved a birthday like this one.

Mr Baines put down his broom. His usually red face was pale. His hair stood on end, and his jersey was a map of smeared party food. He watched, goggling with amazement, as the Stinkwater cats left his house without another sound. Only Darson remained. He watched balefully from the top of the television as the Cockledusters crowded round the body of their King.

'Great Scales!' whispered the dead King's son. 'I'm the King! I'm King Cockleduster the Tenth! My father's finally gone to the country!'

'A terrible loss,' said Biffy. 'But comfort yourself with this, Your Majesty – he died as he lived.'

'Eating,' said the new King.

'No, Sire!' Biffy said a little snappishly. 'I meant that he died leading his cats into battle.'

'Oh, yes,' said the new King Cockleduster. 'Pity we didn't win.'

'Shut up, Cockie!' said the new Queen Bing. 'Maybe we didn't win – but we didn't lose, either.' She drew herself up proudly. 'Darson Stinkwater, we will meet tomorrow dark at Woshnab Marshes.'

'Agreed,' Darson said. Cat noticed that he looked a little bewildered. Something in the room was different. Cat suddenly realized there was no smell of Stinkwater wickedness.

And just as she thought this, she heard Darson whisper to himself, 'Why can't I smell them?'

Mrs Baines wailed, 'Trevor, that cat's DEAD! There's a dead cat on my best table. Take it away!'

Mr Baines blundered through the cats to read the disc on the old King's collar. 'It's that big brute I caught stealing pizza out of the dustbin. He belongs to the Watsons – and they're welcome to him.'

The dead warrior-King was carried back to his land on a shovel. Mr Baines grunted with the effort of supporting the royal weight. The old King's striped tail hung limply, majestic even in death. Mr Baines couldn't understand why the other cats followed him out of the house and seemed to form a solemn procession around him.

'I must be going mad,' Cat heard him whisper to himself.

Just after the funeral-shovel left the Baines's house, a police car arrived. Cat hung back curiously, trying to hear what Mrs Baines was saying.

'. . . at least TWO HUNDRED cats − they attacked us − scratched my daughter − and look at my house! I want you to take their owners' names and have them all put down!'

'What cats, Madam?'

'They've gone − all of a sudden they just turned round and left − oh, why didn't you get here sooner?'

Lucy thought this might be a good moment to go home. She squeezed past Mrs Baines and the two policemen.

'Thanks for having me,' she mumbled. It sounded silly in the circumstances, but she couldn't think of anything else to say.

Her ankle hurt. Her tights were torn, and sticking to the bloody scratches. The small ginger cat who was

Cat had broken away from the procession and was waiting at her front gate.

Lucy hurried to pick her up. 'I know why you didn't stay with Biffy,' she said. 'You couldn't bear to see the poor old Watsons when Mr Baines brings them their dead cat. I can't either. Let's go inside.'

As she had done before, Lucy told Dad that Cat was already upstairs. This time, Cat's observant Mum was beside him. 'Lucy, what have you done to your leg? I'll find the big plasters—'

'Thanks, I'm fine,' Lucy said, hurrying up the stairs to Cat's room.

When the bedroom door had been shut behind them, Cat flung herself on the Professor's stone and changed back into a girl. There were red scratches on her nude human body and a sticky patch of chocolate across her back. She grabbed her dressing gown.

As she whisked it around her, she knocked the alabaster stone off the bed. It fell on the wooden floor with an ominous 'Crack!'

Cat and Lucy stared at each other in absolute horror. There was a long, sickening silence.

'I've broken it!' moaned Cat. 'How could I be so clumsy? I've smashed the stone, and now it won't work – but I MUST be a cat again.' She started to cry.

'You don't know that it won't work,' Lucy said reasonably. She knelt down on the floor to examine the pieces. 'It's a neat break. We can probably – hang on!'

Suddenly, she was excited. 'Cat, you've got to look at this!'

Cat stopped crying and knelt down beside Lucy. One end of the alabaster stone had fallen off.

'It's not solid,' Lucy said. 'It's hollow, like a sort of box – and there's something inside it.' She passed the hollow stone to Cat. 'It's yours, so you do the looking.'

Cat could hardly breathe. Would it be treasure, like a jewel or a piece of gold? Or did the box hold something gross and horrid? She vaguely remembered Dad telling her that Ancient Egyptians had spiked their treasures with deadly diseases, to punish thieves. Her hands shaking, she tipped the hollow stone. Into her palm dropped –

'This is crazy!' gasped Lucy. 'I don't believe it! What's going on?'

The thing inside the Professor's stone was – unmistakably – the Blessed Sardine.

'But the Sardine got torn to shreds and flushed down the toilet,' protested Cat. 'We SAW. And there can't be two of them!'

Lucy eyes gleamed. 'Cat, you're a genius, and you don't even know it.'

'Eh?'

'Your Professor said there were TWO Temple Keys!'

'So?' It took Cat a few seconds to catch up. 'Are you

saying the cats' Sardine was the other Key to the Temple?'

'Of course!' cried Lucy. 'Look – it's identical.' She gently took the mummified fish from Cat's hand. 'The question is, how did a bunch of domestic cats get their paws on something from Ancient Egypt? It doesn't make sense. Cats don't go on holiday and buy souvenirs.'

'Perhaps they robbed a museum,' suggested Cat.

'But you said the Cockledusters got the Sardine hundreds of years ago. They didn't have proper museums in those days.' Lucy slipped the alternative Sardine back inside the hollow stone. She fixed the end with a piece of Sellotape. The stone looked as good as new.

Cat felt the magic tingling up her arm the minute she touched it. 'I'm glad it's still working – I can't wait to show this to Biffy!'

'I don't think it will make much difference,' Lucy said. 'The Stinkwaters saw the Blessed Sardine being destroyed. They'll know that's not the real one.'

Cat asked, 'What should I do with it, then?'

'Be careful,' Lucy said. 'We've seen the power of this thing. I'm not sure we should let the cats mess about with it.'

Later that night, Cat attended a magnificent Sending-Shout for the King in the Watsons' back garden. It was followed by the Coronation-Scratches of the new King and Queen. There was a charming new Sardine-Shouter (Dr Stoffit, a tortoiseshell from the Windy Terribles) and everything went beautifully.

'They're still sure the Sardine will help them to thrash the Stinkwaters,' Cat told Lucy on the way to school next morning. 'The fact that it's in pieces in the sewer doesn't seem to bother them at all. And they're still refusing to budge an inch – they won't make peace with the Stinkwaters on any terms.'

'Silly creatures,' Lucy said, not unkindly.

'The Cockledusters can't forget about Crasho and Vartha,' Cat said. 'And neither can the Stinkwaters. They'll never agree.'

That night, Biffy woke her for the meeting at Woshnab Marshes – the cattish name for a long garage roof behind the pub. The late nights were starting to catch up with Cat, and she was giddy with sleepiness as she trotted along in the crowd of cats. If any humans had been awake, they would have seen something remarkable. Every single cat in the neighbourhood was running through the streets towards the Admiral Tunnock.

For the first time, Cockleduster and Stinkwater cats were meeting in peace, under a flag of truce. And as they crowded on to the garage roof, the two sides looked at each other, and made the great discovery that they weren't so different. When their furry faces

 185

were not distorted with hatred, Stinkwaters looked very much like Cockledusters. They also smelt very much like their old enemies. This caused confusion, and it took the two sides a long time to sort themselves out. Cat sat on Biffy's back (which was like a very warm, slippery sofa), so that she could see over the forest of pointed ears.

The new King and Queen faced Darson and Sleeza.

'Neither of us has the Blessed Sardine,' said Darson. 'Neither of us can use its powers. So I suggest we stop this war and keep our borders as they are.'

All friendliness between the two sides vanished. Hisses and snarls ran through the crowd of cats.

'Of all the cheek!' fumed Queen Bing. 'What about the Cockleduster lands you STOLE during this war? You give them back!'

'Not until you give me back my daughter!' screeched Sleeza.

'What are you talking about?' yelled Queen Bing. 'Your scarlap daughter stole MY SON. Release him at once!'

'My Vartha is NOT a scarlap! Your Crasho is just a plapp and a tumfrit!'

'He is NOT!'

'He IS!'

Cat was anxious. The Cockledusters and the Stinkwaters had starting trading insults. Fights broke out across the crowded roof. Biffy was growling deep in his chest. This was no way to end the war.

'Ladies, ladies,' a peculiar, cattish voice cut in suddenly, 'this fighting must end!'

Something about this voice made the cats uneasy. Silence fell. A black figure walked fearlessly into the middle of the crowd.

'Wizewun!' Cat cried, surprised. 'What are you doing here?'

'Girlcat,' said Queen Bing, 'do you know this creature? I have never seen him, in your land or ours. And yet he doesn't seem to be a Crudge.'

'He's not, your majesty,' Cat said (knowing that 'Crudge' was what domestic cats called the wild ones). 'He lives at the wild camp.'

Mews and whispers ran through the watching cats. They were afraid of the wild ones.

'So you're the new King and Queen,' Wizewun said. 'And you two must be the principle Stinkwaters. I have some news for you.'

There was a bulky piece of plastic bag fastened to Wizewun's collar. With great neatness, he pulled it out with one back leg and laid it at the paws of Bing and Sleeza. He opened out the plastic with his teeth.

Bing and Sleeza screamed.

He had brought two small collars – one green, one red.

'That's Vartha's!' cried Sleeza.

'That's Crasho's!' cried Queen Bing. 'Where did you find these? Have you news of my son?'

'I'm very, very sorry, your majesty,' Wizewun said solemnly. 'I'm very sorry, Mrs Sleeza. These two young cats hid at my home in the wild camp, because they had no other refuge. Their families had turned against them. But their only crime was falling in love.' His yellow-green eyes swept over all the silent, staring, frightened cats. 'And now these lovers are no more! They have found the country where they can be together for ETERNITY.'

'DEAD!' sobbed Sleeza and Bing. The two mothers burst into mews of pain and sorrow that cut into every cattish heart like daggers.

'Dead!' echoed Darson, his shaking voice a shadow of itself. 'My little Vartha – my daffodil!'

'My Crasho!' wailed Queen Bing. 'My fluffy kitten! The first one of his litter to climb out of the box!'

All the cats were crying now – including Cat, who had always felt so sorry for the doomed lovers.

'These two young cats,' said Wizewun, 'should have met and loved and married in peace – a small enough thing to ask in this rough world. Instead, they were forced to run away and live in the wild. I did what I could for them. But yesterday they were crushed under a falling heap of rubbish. Look at these two Plinky collars and WEEP! They were killed by this stupid war. If the Cockledusters and Stinkwaters had stuck to their own lands, these innocent cats would be alive today!'

This was a terrible lesson. The cats wept. Cat thought how small and pathetic the two collars looked on the tarry surface of the garage roof.

Darson said, 'My Vartha was the light of our land. If it could bring her back, I'd happily end this war.'

'I wouldn't care who Crasho married,' sobbed Bing, 'if I could only lick him one more time.'

Wizewun was calm and stern. 'The best memorial you can give these lovers is PEACE.'

'Yes,' cried Sleeza, 'let there be peace. I can't fight any more!'

'Poor thing,' Biffy muttered, with unexpected sympathy. 'Terrible to lose a kitten!'

Out in the silent night a beautiful cat voice began to sing a lament. More voices joined in, until a whole choir of cats mewed and howled at the sky. With a shiver, Cat recognized the mysterious music of the wild cats.

'Our wild brothers,' Wizewun said, 'are carrying back the dead bodies.'

'Then we will make the Peace-Scratches,' Darson said brokenly. 'This strange cat is right – their blood is on our paws.'

The singing of the wild cats came closer. Cat was near enough the edge of the roof to see them in the alley below. She caught her breath – no human would

 189

have believed this astonishing sight. A procession of wild cats, all singing a heart-rending funeral howl, walked slowly towards Woshnab Marshes. They were pushing a large and rather mouldy cardboard box, on what appeared to be the wheels of an old buggy. The Plinkies watched in silence as the sad procession halted.

Wizewun suddenly smiled. 'Now there is peace between you,' he said, 'let there be JOY!' He waved his paw at the wild cats below.

The lid of the cardboard box popped open, to reveal the grinning head of Prince Crasho. 'Hello, Mother! Hello, Father!'

'My BOY!' screamed the Queen. 'Can I believe my nose? Is this a GHOST?'

A pretty black and brown head bobbed up beside Crasho. 'Will you forgive us, Father? Will you accept Crasho as your son?'

'Of course he will!' shouted Sleeza, doing a somersault of happiness. All the parents rushed down to the street. There were head-buttings and lickings – the cat version of hugs and kisses. Queen Bing graciously licked Vartha, and the whole garage roof broke into silent purring cheers. The two warring families were officially united.

Vartha beckoned Sleeza and Bing over to the box and threw open the lid.

All the Plinkies cried, 'AAAAAAH!'

For nestling inside the box, on a heap of Wizewun's mattress-stuffing, lay four tiny kittens – three brown-and-white, one pure black. Their eyes were shut, and they squeaked for milk like baby birds. The two proud grandmothers forgot they were enemies and covered the kittens with licks.

'Two boys and two girls,' said Crasho. He introduced them. 'Prince Trumble, Princess Cockina, Prince Woop and Princess Darsonetta! You see, we named our daughters after both our fathers – these kittens are Cockledusters AND Stinkwaters!'

Cat felt ridiculously happy. The war was over, and love had triumphed. Woshnab Marshes was a carnival of celebration. Mackerella joined her splendid voice to the singing. Major Mincible proposed to the shy Princess Tarba. The jilted Countess Ploshkin proposed to one of Darson's guards. Larfing Silex proposed to Spikeletta's youngest daughter. There were so many proposals between Cockledusters, Stinkwaters and wild cats that Dr Stoffit was shouting Wedding-Scratches until sunrise.

Cat found herself on the fringes of the furry crowd, beside Wizewun.

'You're so clever,' she said admiringly. 'How did you think of pretending the runaways were dead? How did you know it would work?'

Wizewun chuckled. 'I simply remembered my Shakespeare – he was always pulling stunts like that.'

Through her happiness, Cat felt a sudden chill of alarm. 'Hang on,' she said, 'cats don't know about Shakespeare! Who are you?'

As soon as the words were out of her mouth, she realized she had given herself away. Wizewun stared at her in silence for a long time. Then he said, 'I might as well ask — who are YOU?'

An orange street light nearby brought out the odd shape of his furry cheekbones. At that moment, Cat was suddenly reminded of a photograph Dad kept on his desk.

She blurted out, 'Professor Katzenberg!'

14
tHE tRUtH ABOUt WiZEWUN

Never had she seen a cat look so astonished.
Wizewun's furry lips moved for several minutes
before he could make a sound.

'You – you KNOW me!' he whispered.

'Then you are Professor Katzenberg?'

'I WAS,' said Wizewun. 'What about you? You're
obviously a human too – so how on earth did you
turn into a cat?'

Cat was surprised that he didn't know. 'It was the
stone you sent to my dad – the Temple Key.'

'Your dad?' Wizewun was puzzled. 'I sent the stone
to Julian Williams, my favourite old student. But his
daughter's a baby.'

'I grew up,' Cat said, smiling. 'I'm nearly eleven
now.'

'Eleven! Good grief, how time flies. How did you know how to change into a cat?'

'I didn't,' Cat said. 'It was a mistake.' As briefly as possible, she told Wizewun the whole story.

He listened very seriously, his black head on one side. 'Fascinating!' he said, when she had finished. 'Well done, Miss Williams – I can see that you'll be an even better student than your father. And he was the best human student I ever had.'

Cat was touched by this praise of Dad. 'He thinks you're dead,' she said.

The old cat sighed sadly. 'Oh dear. I was afraid of that. How did they think I'd died?'

'Eaten by crocodiles.'

'Hmmm, not bad. But the truth is even more bizarre. Well, how are your parents?'

'Very well,' Cat said, thinking how odd it felt to have a cat asking after your parents. 'Dad still misses you. He made a lovely speech at your funeral.'

'Good old Julian!' Wizewun's voice wobbled. He cleared his throat. 'I wish there was some way I could send him my regards. Impossible, of course.'

Cat's mind was teeming with questions. 'You died – I mean, disappeared – in Egypt. So what are you doing here? Are you a sort of ghost?'

'Heavens, no!' smiled Wizewun, 'I'm as alive as you are. I'll tell you my story, but I'd rather not do it here – if my wild ones find out I used to be human, they'll kill me. Come back to my oil-drum. I'll make sure you get home safely.'

The two human cats left the party and flitted through the streets to the old railway. Wizewun led Cat to his hidden house among the weeds. They settled comfortably on the mattress-stuffing, and he began his incredible story.

Katzenberg's Tale

I freely admit that before I disappeared I was obsessed with the legend of Pahnkh, and disgustingly greedy for the fabled treasure. Your father thought I'd gone dangerously mad (on our last dig, I kept looking round to find him creeping up behind me with a syringe), but I was saner than I had ever been – and I was about to make the discovery of my career.

Let me remind you of the details. The god-cat left two Keys to his magical Temple. After a lifetime of research into Pahnkh, I had learned that both the Keys, used in a certain way, would let a person into the Chamber of Gold. Well, the last time I went to Egypt, I found one of the Temple Keys. Nobody else believed in it, but I knew it proved the legend was true. I knew that if I used the Key to change myself into a cat, I would easily find the other Key – and then I would be rich. So I spent all my savings on the white alabaster stone.

You seem to have managed your transformation

with enviable ease. I had to work at turning myself into a cat that first time.

My first successful transformation took place in my hotel room. What an interesting experience! When you are an adult, Miss Williams, I hope you'll write a book about it — it will certainly change the face of Egyptology. As you know, becoming a cat feels wonderful. I chased spiders and ran up the curtains for ages. More importantly, I found that I could read certain scratches on an ancient piece of ivory. They were cat writing, and gave me my first real clue — the location of an ancient cat graveyard on the banks of the Nile. The other Key must be here, I thought.

I prepared carefully for my search. In case anything happened, I left a letter for your father, and instructions that all my belongings should be sent to him (I thought he was still working at the University of Skegness, so I'm very glad it eventually reached your new house).

I put the alabaster stone in my pocket, and took a train and a taxi to the place on the river bank. I changed myself into a cat and began my search. But it was here that everything started to go wrong. I had wandered rather a long way from my heap of clothes when I met my fate — in the shape of two British tourists called Mr and Mrs Everbott.

Now, I don't want to be too mean about the Everbotts. They were kind, well-meaning people.

They didn't know — how could they? — that they were ruining all my plans. You see, they thought I was a stray and they were full of pity for me. Mrs Everbott cried over me and (I'm sorry to say) kept kissing me.

I struggled and protested, but it didn't do any good. The Everbotts dragged me back to their hotel room. It was terrible that I couldn't explain. I shouted my head off, but all they heard were mews. I was furious — but Mrs Everbott didn't know she was really kissing and stroking a bald old Professor.

There was no escape. My heart lifted when I saw them packing their suitcases — at last, I thought, I shall be free again.

But then everything went BLACK.

I don't know how long I was unconscious. I woke up in what looked like a prison cell. It was actually a pet-carrier with metal bars. I was in an English car, passing English road signs — and there in the front were Mr and Mrs Everbott.

'Ooh, look!' cried Mrs Everbott. 'He's awake! Don't worry, Button — we'll get you home safe and sound.'

Mr Everbott gave me a rather sour look in the mirror. 'Let's hope he's worth it. That animal nearly got us both arrested.'

I later found out that foolish Mrs Everbott had DRUGGED me and smuggled me home on the plane, so I wouldn't have to go into quarantine for six months. She MEANT to be kind — but my Temple

Key was in Egypt, and I was on the outskirts of Watford. What on earth was I supposed to do?

'How dare you call me Button!' I stormed. 'For the last time, my name is Professor Sigmund Katzenberg!' Useless, of course. She just poked a cat treat through my bars. I was well and truly TRAPPED.

The Everbotts had a nice enough house. They treated me like a king, and I must admit I was gloriously comfortable. I had a basket, a duvet, a bowl with 'Button' on it and three different collars to match Mrs Everbott's moods. I was warm and well fed, but I wasn't happy. I was so dreadfully bored without my human work. I was lonely, too – the local cats were all spoilt Plinkies, and very dull company. I had to get away.

My only hope was that your father had got my Temple Key. But I didn't know how to contact him – I knew that he could have left Skegness by now. I decided I had to get to London, to find a man named Horace Venables. Professor Venables taught me at university, and he also taught your father. He's bound to have Julian's address, I told myself. I hadn't seen old Venables in years, and I hoped he was still alive.

My chance came when I heard Mr Everbott saying he was driving down to London. I jumped into the boot when he wasn't looking. I knew I wouldn't have any trouble giving him the slip – he wasn't as fond of me as his wife was, and would probably be glad to see the back of me.

It was a long journey. Mr Everbott was taking a haddock to his mother, and I'm afraid I ate it. He was very cross when he opened the boot and found me.

'You!' he said. 'Why you little – !' Well, I won't repeat it exactly.

My tail got caught and I couldn't get out. But Mr Everbott pulled me out and dropped me on the pavement. 'Go on,' he said, 'you just (something) off!'

And I was a free cat.

After several days of eating out of dustbins and trying to read street signs, I dragged my aching paws up the front path of 14 Tidbury Gardens, the home of Venables.

'Professor!' I shouted. 'It's Sigmund Katzenberg! Let me in!'

It came out as a hungry mew, but it did the trick. A very old man with white hair opened the door – my dear old Professor. Luckily for me he liked cats, and he kindly adopted me. I started hunting for your father's address the next day. The old gentleman lived all alone, in a house stuffed with all kinds of crazy objects. I couldn't find any addresses – but I did find something else.

It was a photograph of Venables, taken in Egypt in the 1930s. While I was lingering over it to laugh at his shorts, I noticed that he was holding a distinctive white stone. Yes! It had to be – it could only be – THE OTHER TEMPLE KEY! It was hidden somewhere in this house! I spent the next few weeks turning that house upside-down — and found nothing.

Venables had an old-fashioned typewriter in his sitting room. One evening, when the two of us were having our warm milk beside the gas fire, I had an idea. I went to the typewriter. Again and again, I tapped the letter 'H' with my paw.

Eventually, Venables noticed. 'What is it, Button?' he asked (alas, I had this awful name appended to my collar). 'Why do you keep patting the 'H'?'

I had his attention. I reached out my little paw and tapped another letter.

'E,' said Venables.

It was working!

Laboriously, I spelled out 'HELLO VENABLES".

Well, the poor old man nearly died of shock — I felt bad about that. But over several evenings I managed to spell out my story. At last, Venables knew who I was and why I needed that Temple Key.

'So it was all true!' the old boy mused. 'The Temple did exist — and the prehistoric Cult of Pahnkh. But I'm terribly sorry, Sigmund — I don't have that Key any more.'

Didn't have it! I let out a miaow that anyone could tell was a groan of despair.

'You see,' said Venables, 'it was smashed during the Blitz. It turned out to have a small, mummified fish inside it. I gave it to my cat to play with.'

This, as you will have guessed, was the origin of the Blessed Sardine. That cat must have discovered something amazing about the fish — lord knows what — which caused the Cockleduster cats to worship it down the generations. Cats and humans have different concepts of time — one of our years is seven cat-years. That's what led to your confusion about the age of the Blessed Sardine. The War with the Birds didn't happen hundreds of years ago. It's the cat name for the Second World War — they think it was caused by huge metal birds who dropped fireballs (well, cats do tend to blame birds for everything).

Anyway, the Temple Key and the Sardine were one and the same. I asked questions in the neighbourhood, but the local cats were very suspicious and told me nothing. I resigned myself to living as a cat. As the months went by, I realized that I liked it. Old Venables and I were very happy together. I more or less looked after him at the end — I found I could switch the kettle on with my teeth, and work the toaster. We spent many a happy evening over the typewriter, talking about the old days.

When he died, I didn't want another human. I built my house here, and the wild ones learned to trust me. They are amazing creatures — nobody really understands them. When Prendergast used Spikeletta to hide the stolen Sardine, Spikeletta respected me enough to offer it to me — not for nothing, naturally,

 201

but at a knock-down price. But I decided that I didn't want it. My wild ones need me. I'm happier now than I have ever been in my life.

You tell me now, Miss Williams, that I have just missed my chance to unite the Keys and enter the Chamber. I could have been the richest man in the world – but I find that I don't care. I've found more true riches here, with my wild ones, than I ever did among the humans.

'What an adventure!' Cat said, when Wizewun had finished. She couldn't help wondering what it would be like to have both Sardines and become fabulously rich. But something in the idea made her uneasy, and deep down she knew no good could ever come of Pahnkh's treasure. 'I expect you'll write a book about it, as soon as you're a human again.'

'Oh, I'll never be human again,' Wizewun said.

'But Professor, I've got your Temple Key. You can come right home with me – Dad'll get such a surprise in the morning.'

Before Wizewun could reply, the tall weeds around the oil-drum rustled. A pretty little wild she-cat poked her head into the clearing.

'Don't worry,' said Wizewun, 'it's only my eleventh wife. I'll be with you in a minute, dear.'

The she-cat nodded and vanished back into the weeds.

Wizewun looked a little embarrassed. He licked his paw. 'I can see that I've surprised you.'

'I thought you'd be dying to change back into a human,' Cat said. 'Do you mean you actually PREFER being a cat? For EVER?'

'Look at it from my point of view,' said Wizewun. 'What can the human world offer me? My career was in ruins. I'd spent all my money. As a human, I was never attractive to women and never had a girlfriend. As a cat, I seem to be an absolute pin-up. They're queuing up to marry me! I've had to start a waiting list.'

'So you won't be coming home with me.' Cat was disappointed – she had been looking forward to Dad's joy when he discovered Katzenberg was alive.

Wizewun smiled, and stroked the top of her head with his paw. 'Don't be sad, Miss Williams. Tell your father you had a lovely dream about me, in which I assured you that I was very happy – only you'd better leave out the eleven wives.'

'OK.'

'And don't forget to tell him he should be very proud of his daughter. I never dreamed that you would be able to use the stone so easily. Obviously, you have a natural flair for this kind of work. When you grow up, you must be the one to write the book about all this. Now,' he stood up briskly, 'I must walk you home before the sun comes up.'

Cat asked, 'May I come and see you again?'

'Take my advice,' Wizewun said. 'Don't turn yourself into a cat again.'

This startled Cat. 'What, never? Why?'

'That black face you see when you use the key,' Wizewun said, 'belongs to Pahnkh.'

'I thought it must be Pahnkh. He looks so wise!'

'He's very crafty,' Wizewun said. 'But he wasn't a good leader to the Ancient Egyptians — well, would you take orders from a cat? Now that he is nearly forgotten and his Temple is silent, he has nothing to do except make trouble. When Venables's cat got hold of the Sardine during the War, he must have done something to wake the sleeping god. Since then, I suspect, Pahnkh has kept up this cat war simply for his own amusement.'

Cat remembered the end of the battle at Emily's party. 'Did he do something with the cats' smells?'

'Well done, Miss Williams! Yes, Pahnkh made each side smell of wickedness to the other. It could have carried on for years. Luckily, a force far stronger than Pahnkh took over.'

'What force?'

Wizewun smiled dreamily. 'Love,' he said. 'That's all it took. Pahnkh felt his power slipping as soon as Crasho and Vartha fell in love. When one Sardine was destroyed, his power just melted away. I doubt he'll be bothering the Plinkies of Bagwell Park again.'

'If Pahnkh's gone,' Cat said, 'doesn't that make it safe for me to turn back into a cat?'

'I'm sorry.' Wizewun's voice was gentle. 'It may be safer now, but it's still not advisable. After a while, the cat would start to affect the human in you — look what happened to me. And cats aren't entirely suitable company for a ten-year-old girl. As you've seen, they do have their limitations.'

Cat bowed her marmalade head. She would miss being the girlcat, but in her heart, she knew Wizewun was right. Every time she turned into a cat, more cattishness flooded into her brain. And every time she mixed with cats, she seemed to stay longer. She had already noticed cattish changes in her human self — the previous day she had found herself wanting to torture a pigeon, just for the fun of it. One day, if she wasn't careful, she might forget to turn back altogether. And, unlike Professor Katzenberg, she preferred being a human.

'Cheer up,' Wizewun said kindly. 'You'll see me around the neighbourhood, and I'll always let you stroke me. One day, when you and your parents are sitting in your garden, I might pop in to join you. You mustn't say who I am. But you'll know — and you'll know that I'm always looking out for you.'

'You've been so kind to me,' Cat said. 'Is there anything I can bring you, as a thank-you present?'

'A packet of Meaty Sticks would be nice,' said

 205

Wizewun. 'I can still appreciate a Plinky treat. And maybe you could get me a small chess set, so I can start teaching the more intelligent wild ones. After all, I'm going to have a lot of time on my paws, now the neighbourhood cats have started living in peace.'

Cat and Lucy went to buy the chess set and the Meaty Sticks next Saturday morning – the first morning of the summer holidays. Mum had booked Cat and Lucy into an activity week at a big house in the country called Pofton Hall. It was the sort of thing Cat would once have dreaded (Mum kept saying, 'Are you SURE you want to go?') but knowing she would have a best friend beside her made it seem thrilling and fun. The activities included rock-climbing and canoeing, and her cat experience had given Cat a taste for this kind of cattish activity. It had left her body with a cat-like itch to climb and leap and throw herself into adventures. She and Lucy still had tons to talk about, but nowadays cat business took second place.

Emily Baines was sitting on the wall outside her house.

'She's always hanging about,' Cat said scornfully.

'We can just hurry past,' Lucy said.

Cat sighed, and shook her head. 'I can't. I still feel terrible about ruining her party.' She arranged her face into what she hoped was a friendly expression. 'Hi!' she called.

To her surprise, Emily smiled and said, 'Hi.'

The two girls walked over to Emily.

'Lucy told me about your party,' Cat said. 'I saw the picture of your wrecked sofa in the *Bagwell Park Courier*. It must have been horrible. I – I hope everything's all right now.'

Even more surprisingly, Emily went on smiling. 'It was a bit scary at the time, but everything's fine now. Mum's really pleased, because the insurance company has given her money for a new sofa and new curtains. She loves decorating.'

'What about your dad?' Lucy asked.

'Well, he started off really angry,' Emily said, 'because it was so hard to get anyone to believe him. But when they did believe him, all sorts of cat experts came and looked at our house to find out what made the local cats behave like that. And my dad got more and more fascinated by cat behaviour. He's nearly an expert himself now.' She turned to Lucy. 'Your cat died, didn't it?'

'Yes,' Lucy said, rather stiffly.

But Emily was not preparing for one of her insults. She only asked if Lucy was interested in getting another cat. 'Because the people at Number 7 have got some GORGEOUS kittens!'

Cat gave Lucy a secret nudge. Number 7 was the land of Vartha Stinkwater.

'It was rather strange,' Emily went on innocently.

'Apparently their cat disappeared for days and then suddenly turned up again – with four babies!'

Cat and Lucy made interested noises. Cat didn't dare to look at Lucy, in case she burst out laughing.

'Marcus at the pub's taken one of them,' Emily went on. 'Because poor Widnes obviously isn't coming back. And guess what – just a minute!' She jumped up and dashed into her house. Cat and Lucy exchanged shrugs and waited.

Emily reappeared with her father. Mr Baines's hands were cupped together. He was holding something in them, very carefully.

'Here's the new arrival, girls,' he said cheerfully. 'We haven't given him a name yet.'

The three girls crowded round him. His big hands gently cradled an adorable fat kitten. The kitten opened his blue eyes and sneezed.

Without thinking, Cat cried, 'It's Prince Trumble!' Lucy nudged her sharply, and Cat blushed dark red. The Baineses would think she was crazy.

'Trumble?' Emily echoed. 'That's it! Oh Dad, can we call him Trumble? Please?'

Mr Baines laughed. 'Why not? It does seem to suit him.'

Emily stroked the tiny brown-and-white head with one finger. 'Trumble. I'm going to miss him at Pofton Hall.'

Cat and Lucy exchanged looks of alarm.

'Rubbish,' Emily's dad said, 'you'll be far too busy having a great time.'

'I won't know anybody,' Emily said disconsolately.

'You'll know us,' Lucy said. 'We're going to the activity week at Pofton Hall. Me and Cat.'

Emily was nervous. Cat could imagine what was going through her mind. At Pofton Hall she would be without her gang. If Cat and Lucy were her enemies, they could make the activity week a total nightmare. But if the Cockledusters and the Stinkwaters could be friends, why not Cat and Emily? She found herself giving Emily a reassuring grin.

'It's going to be fantastic,' she said.

'There you are!' beamed Mr Baines. Since the final battle, he had been far nicer and less shouty. 'You'll have two school friends with you. What could be better? Now, I must take young Trumble back inside. See you, girls.'

Cat and Lucy said goodbye and hurried round the corner.

'Good grief,' Cat said. 'I'm going on an activity week with nasty Emily Baines – why don't I mind?'

'Because you've both realized it's in your best interests to be friends,' Lucy said. 'Just like the cats.'

'Yes, I was just thinking exactly the same thing,' Cat said. 'The Stinkwaters managed to stop being evil – maybe Emily will be the same.'

Lucy smiled. 'Where cats leads, humans follow.

 209

Look at these two – at Pofton Hall, that will be you and Emily Baines!'

She pointed to the middle of the road. Side by side, their tails and heads held high, strolled General Biffy and Darson Stinkwater.

Cat laughed. 'Yes, if Biffy can be friends with Darson, anything's possible!'

How happily it had all ended, she thought. In just a few days there were hardly any differences between Cockledusters and Stinkwaters – losing the Blessed Sardine seemed to have done wonders for feline harmony. Now Darson would be living with his own grandson. The kittens of Crasho and Vartha were already little symbols of unity.

'I wonder what Darson and Biffy say to each other,' Lucy mused. 'Have you really given up being a cat? Aren't you ever tempted to do it just one more time?'

Cat shook her head. 'I missed it a lot at first. But after a few days the cattish side of me started to fade – maybe the magic wears off when you don't use it. And I can see now that the Professor was right, I might have got addicted to cattishness and forgotten how to be human.'

'I suppose being human does have its points,' Lucy said.

'Oh yes,' Cat said firmly. 'It's loads more fun being a girl.'

The alabaster stone, with the one surviving Sardine

inside it, was carefully wrapped in an old silk scarf and hidden at the very bottom of her underwear drawer. Cat wasn't intending to turn into a cat again, and she told herself that she was only keeping the stone in case Professor Katzenberg changed his mind. But sometimes, when she caught a thousand cattish scents on an evening breeze, or sensed the tingling ends of phantom whiskers on her face, she remembered how wonderful it had felt to be a cat, and knew deep down that she would be a cat again.

GLOSSARY OF tHE CAt LANGUAGE

Crudge . . . . A wild cat

Dogplop . . . . Term of abuse (very self explanatory)

Droopag . . . . A foolish elderly female

Krebbins . . . . Term of abuse or expletive (very vulgar); also see **Skugg, Squett, Stigg**

Plapp . . . . Idiot (very vulgar)

Plinky . . . . Wild cat term for a domestic cat

Scarlap . . . . An unscrupulous young female

Skugg . . . . Very rude form of abuse

Squett . . . . See above

Stigg . . . . See above

Tumfrit . . . . Coward or weakling (a particularly strong insult)

Wingthing . . . . A butterfly

Woodle-foodle . . . . . . Nonsense, nonsensical

 213